MW00712910

UNCOMPROMISING:

FAMILY STYLE

A New Novel by

Elizabeth Lydia Bodner

To Pam
All the Best
Elizabeth

EBW Associates
South Portland, ME

ISBN: 0-9657162-0-1

Library of Congress Card Catalog No. 97-090128

Grateful acknowledgement is made to the following for permission
to reprint previously published material:
The Selected Poetry of Ranier Maria Rilke
Edited and translated by Stephen Mitchell
Vintage International, A division of Random House Inc., NY

This book is a work of fiction.
Certain real locations, products and public figures are mentioned
but all other characters and the events and dialogue
described in the book are from the author's imagination.

Edited by William Appel, Edit Ink
172 Holtz Drive, Cheektowaga, NY 14225

Manufactured in the United States of America

EBW Associates
PO Box 2809
South Portland, ME 04116

DEDICATION

This book is dedicated to all of our families through compromises and uncompromises. Without our foundation, our house would fall.

First and foremost to my wonderful lifetime companion
and dearest love, James Cumiskey

A pet companion, Geoffrey of Orange,
a beautiful tabby who sat and slept nearby
keeping me company unconditionally.

Generous and kind librarians in the cities in which we have lived:
Downers Grove Public Library, Downers Grove, Illinois
Richland Public Library, Richland, Washington

And most of all to the people in the great state of Maine, in which independence of individuals flourishes and where this publication came to completion:

Julie Zimmerman, Audenreed Press
Irene Howe, coordinator
Middy Thomas, cover illustration

TABLE OF CONTENTS

UNCOMPROMISING:

FAMILY STYLE

Chapter 1 A Dapper Man

He was said to be the most "dapper" dresser in Eastburgh. And that was a fact. Even Sal said so, and he was the voice of Eastburgh and the local prohibition officer. Johnny was the smoothest talker and dresser he'd ever met, Sal said, and, what's more, he was an athlete. He could kick a football as high as Knute Rockne, even though he wouldn't become a professional football player. He wouldn't become a car salesman either, and that's what he was really good at. Selling at Pop Gesner's Chrysler Garage was his one big joy on summer vacations home from college.

John Aloyisius Albred was slated for big things. Everyone thought so except Lizzie. She wanted him to be a priest. In fact, she sent him to prep school as soon as he turned fourteen to study theology. Johnny was a real rake too. He'd tip his straw hat to the ladies and flash a smile with those rosy cherub cheeks making them tingle all over with excitement.

These were the 1920's, a carefree, hi-flying time when the stock market and skirts were rising, to uneven proportions, and young men, especially Johnny, ogled approvingly. As World War I ended and prosperity and light-hearted hedonism saturated the air, Johnny's social expression became uninhibited as well, while he laughed at the world. He could turn trouble into a joyride, like the time Lizzie saw him riding someone around in the rumble seat of a brand new roadster from Pop's showroom and he quickly pulled a cap from under the seat, cocking it jauntily over his forehead like some "Devil's champion" of the road.

"What did you do all day, John? I see you all the time

happy, riding people around," questioned Lizzie, in her best Czechoslovakian-English.

"I'm selling cars, Ma. The customers want to know what they're buyin', so we go out for a ride and talk, and laugh like we've been friends for years. Ha, especially when they sign on the dotted line. This, my dear mother, is a true sign of friendship."

Motorcars were his life. The new 1925 Chrysler Maxwell Sedan and the Chrysler Six, which sold retail for $1,545, consumed almost all of his interest. Johnny gazed mesmerically at the newly delivered vehicle. "That car is a lulu," he whistled in exaltation. Built of special heat-treated steel with a powerful six-cylinder motor, sliding gear transmission, semi-elliptic front and three quarter elliptic rear springs, mohair top, and thick plush luxuriously upholstered wide seats designated for large capacity. Johnny's love affair for cars began with "The Good Maxwell," that's what they called it then, the day that he and Lizzie walked into Pop's Garage, and their eyes landed on it, The Car. He was the one who did the driving so he picked out a "snazzy" maroon Touring Car with black trim.

"Hey, by the way, you lookin' for a good salesman?" He asked Pop, as he watched the new line of cars being unloaded at the back entrance of the garage.

The marriage was consummated—Pop got a good man out front and Johnny spent summers near his second love, the new motorcar. Warren G. Harding was elected President in 1920 and Johnny, along with nine million private automobiles, taxis, motorcycles, buses and trucks, went chugging along at the "break-neck" speed of 20 mph. Sunday afternoon drives were as pleasant as Sunday dinner, except for the combo-cacophony of horse-drawn hacks, buses, drays, grocers' wagons, bicycles, and clanging trolley cars, some of which were gratefully gone. But hatefully, most stayed, along with noise and air pollution and parking problems and colossal traffic jams and the heightened probability of getting killed in the street by a car or a semi or whatever. None of this bothered the common motorists in their runabouts fetching ten miles at a speed no horse could match. Consequently, John Q. and his family were Johnny's best patrons, even though they favored Model T's once in a while. Johnny would usually snag them on reliability or what a nice vehicle to take the family in to the city to see the latest movies advertised. If the farmer's wife came with him, Johnny usually had a better chance for a sale. She liked to picture herself as Gloria Swanson or Theda Barra. This little glamour note didn't hurt at all, because the "woman of the house" usually planned the town trips to J. C. Penney or Sears & Roebuck Company to buy clothing where the selection was wider and prices lower than the small country stores.

Elizabeth Kuchen Albred, a strong, orderly woman, ran her hotel the way she disciplined her son: Strict. She had a stake in the business and intended to make it work, like she did, from morning until night cleaning, cooking, acting as all around business manager. Commanding her small staff with the authority of the captain of a large seagoing vessel, they were all kept at an even keel. When the waves got rough, she held on to the stern. Amidst this sea of activity, her religious fervor flourished.

Daily Mass was first on her schedule. She climbed the hill to St. Helen's early every morning. Purchasing the bell for Eastburgh's biggest cathedral was only part of her plan for the religious community. She was passionately involved in her son's future in the priesthood.

"Lizzie, Lizzie, my good woman, why don't you let the boy make up his own mind?" Zach would say.

She and Zach were a team, mostly because Zach

preferred to stay quietly in the background tending bar in the restaurant portion of the hotel. Besides, he knew Lizzie to have the courage behind all her convictions. She knew how to put thoughts and dreams into action, challenging all odds to accomplish her goal.

Zach was fifteen years older than she, with black lung from his coal mining days in Hungary. He did only a small amount of physical work, before becoming breathless from exhaustion. By nature, Zach was a relaxed guy who could just let the world roll by from day to day. He saw no sense in why Lizzie hustled all day long in a whirl of activity. Their philosophies were completely different, and this included raising their other two children, Philip and Agatha. Neither child was ever disciplined in any way; each was given freedom to find their own way through life.

Philip was a troublesome boy who was naturally attracted to mischief. Stealing, lying, cheating and major acts of defiance became exciting conquests of everyday life, making the Eastburgh jail his second home. But, Lizzie had an excellent relationship with the police and was on very good terms with the local constable. She paid Philip's fines. In the meantime, after Phil made appropriate promises and helped himself to the available cash in the register, he was once again free to cause trouble. People talked, especially those who were boarders in her hotel.

"Why doesn't Lizzie put some of that religion into Phillie instead of Johnny?"

But not many people said that to Lizzie's face since she could be fearsome in defending her children's welfare, even to the point of taking the broom to some of them. She'd been known to do that whenever they used profanity or spoke without respect to the ladies, herself included.

Phil's latest scheme was bootlegging at night. Driving

a truck that took the corn to the still, he oversaw the operation of transporting the bottles of whiskey to the customers. The whiskey was alcohol diluted with tap water flavored with some juice or creosote for scotch. There was big money in this and Phil planned to go big time.

One of the major stops for Lonnie, Phil's crooked cohort, was the Albred Hotel. The 18th Amendment of 1919 to the Constitution prohibited the manufacture and sale of intoxicating liquor, but most people resented the law, drinking in illegal clubs or "speakeasies". Consequently, the government found it more difficult to enforce prohibition due to public opinion. Also, since grafting politicians, venal police, unscrupulous doctors, bootleggers, moonshiners, homebrewers and rum-runners filtered throughout society, Phil was just another link in the sophisticated chain of its sneakiest celebrities.

Agatha was a natural beauty, whose brain went unexercised. That is not to say she didn't have the biological capability to think. She could be very deceptive when it came to extracting large amounts of money from Lizzie. One of the investments attractive to her might be the latest outfit advertised in Vogue that week. Revising nature, since plump was no longer fashionable, she would force her curvaceous body into the new sleek fashions. The "Boyishform" brassiere set the foundation for this new breed of woman. She read religiously all the fashion and new movie magazines, especially the advertisements. She believed in them, embodied them, such as the new dropped waistline, short skirt and sometimes backless dress. Captivating this latest wardrobe lured her to the local haute couture for her own individual fitting. As she dressed for the evening, Aggie pushed her plump toes into the new long, pointed satin slippers advertised for the surefooted Tango, Fox-Trot, Black Bottom, Shimmy and Charleston dancers, in which she moved with the best of them. A woman of Aggie's stylish splendor was very acceptable, as advertisements carried the message then: Ladies must be beautiful, intelligence is deceitful, amiability is useless, virtue is vain. If you want to please a strong, strenuous, silent male, looks are your only bait—be lovely or lose him. And she was not going to lose him.

The Albred Hotel, reputed to be the best lodging in the area, located ideally across from the new Westinghouse Electric Corporation, was a place where fellow Europeans could congregate. There were mainly Eastern Europeans there, who understood the same language and culture. Czechoslovakians, Hungarians and the like, but there were a few Germans and Irish as well. The melt down throughout the social system was still taking place, as they poured into the country in the early part of the 20th century. These were the people who would be making their integration into society as businessmen, teachers, filtering through various professions as part of a group watering down the so-called true Americans, with their blended-in cultures, languages, and life-styles. They were either integrated or segregated depending upon their social status, breeding, competence, and ability to strategically integrate into an "already in progress" industrialized American system. Upon arrival even with the greatest of these attributes, they then had to be woven into the whole of mainstream society. Looking for daily work and a life of stability, they lined up outside the employment offices ready to apply for work of any kind. Using the hotel as a home base, they waited for word of who was hiring who, when and for how much to reach their sense of economic awareness in a brand new economic system.

A steady flow of surging ambition motivated Lizzie to succeed in her quest as the best hotelier within ten miles of the large industrial center of Pittsburgh. The first of these was to open the restaurant and hotel across from the Westinghouse Electric which attracted many unskilled and skilled immigrants. They settled here primarily because of the hourly wages they were paid. Morning, noon and evening shifts had men coming and going, eating and sleeping there, generating a lucrative and dependable clientele.

These were prosperous times at the hotel. The new borders stepped onto the immaculately clean, white marbled floor shaded by the dark oak paneled dining room and massive brass-lined bar, expecting to find their ethnocentric camaraderie. Soon a cry, a name, a fond nickname rang out, as a relation or village neighbor was spotted from the old country across the room. An embrace would ensue mingled with tears and laughter.

A room rented for ten dollars a week including meals. They were simply furnished but cozy, with a bed, chair and table for writing.

A strong hearty beef stew simmering in a deep black kettle pot on the huge iron stove in the enormous kitchen was generally the first good meal the voyagers shared in their new country. The food was the best in Eastburgh, menus and meals adapted by Lizzie herself. Rising at four o'clock in the morning, she would begin by making raised breads, pies and cakes. Stoking up the big iron stove until it blazed with fury, she thrust heavy metal sheets lined with the first dozen of plump white loaves of dough into huge hot ovens.

The fresh-baked goodness of Lizzie's kitchen sent an aroma all through town, as the people began their day with the conspicuous smell and firm conviction to visit the Albred Hotel for a sample. The Atlantic and Pacific Tea Company Grocery wagons delivered most produce to her door. Newly processed canned goods of every variety stocked neatly in the supply room in the basement. Retail chain operation and massed purchasing power to manufacturing and wholesale meant savings for the consumer. Proprietors encouraged Lizzie to have a credit account, which she discouraged by paying cash only.

Madame Ilona Petrovka had disciplined them back in the old days. She could still hear her engaging voice.

"Elizabeth, bring the gulyas' to a slow simmer, don't forget to put in the parsley roots and an abundance of paprika to the taste, enhancing the flavor. And when you go to the market place, you must demand quality produce.

Madame Petrovka was her mentor, from the elegant city of Budapest. She was the instructor at the local cooking school, where students learned to imitate the master chefs of Europe. Madame had worked in the finest kitchens for the best of dignitaries, including Prince Metternich's royal kitchen staff. Because of her travels, she was respected among all the village people. The fact that she paid particular attention to Elizabeth's adeptness was complementary to the young would-be Chef. Besides encouraging her to ply her craft, Madame helped her to pay closer attention to personal grooming habits in the kitchen. Pulling her long dark hair into a neat plait, Madame wrapped it around the crown of Lizzie's head, framing her round, full face, revealing the rosy cheeked cherub that she appeared to be. Not a natural beauty, Lizzie had a goodness shining from within and glowed with enthusiasm and exuberance for life. Clear hazel eyes projected an all clear signal that everything was fine with the world, and if it wasn't she certainly would find out why. Madame Petrovka favored her because she knew one day Elizabeth would compete in the male-dominated arena to become one of the Master Chef's of Europe or the world. She knew in her heart that Elizabeth needed polish in many areas for developing a professional persona.

As a concentrated and confident student, Lizzie measured and sifted the correct amount of flour into the porcelain bowl to begin the walnut Kalacs recipe, her nimble hands and fingers moved the pliable, soft buttered dough quickly and assuredly, as she molded the rich tasting rolls. "Lizzie," as her classmates called her, was in command in the kitchen, often moving way ahead of the other students. She lifted the delicately flavored Homok Torta out of the oven, while she watched the jeering faces of the young men in her class. They often laughed together in unspoken mockery, though their jealousy may have stemmed from an aura of pomposity encompassing Lizzie that said, "You can't touch me with any derisiveness, I'm naturally-gifted as a food preparer and I will shout it from the mountain tops eventually, If I have to!" The resonance of this impenetrable self-esteem, accelerated their competitive anger with comments like, "Lizzie, you don't have a chance, there is no woman Chef anywhere in the region. Find yourself a good man, have his children and cook for him.

Lizzie was more than aware of the difficulty she would encounter, with realization that hard work with strategy might bring her to some level of importance in this field.

"They will hire me, just the same as you," she exclaimed over the mouth watering vapors.

She had no intention of finding a good man—there was too much to do. Besides, she may even find her future on another continent. Without wasting a moment, she picked up her spatula and began whipping the thick yellow eggs for dumplings. Later, the class would sit down to eat the Turos palacsinta or Crepe-Suzettes with cottage cheese that were made earlier that afternoon.

But now so many years later, sweat glistening on her forehead as she bent over the hot stove, Lizzie also sadly recalled Madame Petrovka divulging to the class about a beating she received for burning a soufflé while working in the kitchen of Franz Joseph. She began to wonder about those circumstances and the kind of conditions that would warrant this harsh punishment. It frightened her to think that an ill-prepared menu could cause such consternation among the rich, privileged classes. She deplored the destruction of Madame's high bred demeanor she had to endure to become accomplished. Now, in her old age, she taught a cooking class in Room No. 1 of the old village police station.

When Lizzie was not in the cooking class she attended five hours twice a week, she worked with her father and brothers on their farm. Working as hard as they, the chicken pen was her exclusive responsibility, from bringing in the fresh straw and mash in the morning to throwing the scratch and collecting the eggs in the afternoon. The family harvested large barrels of wheat, barley, sugar beets, corn and fodder crops. Her mother believed that Lizzie had something special but was not exactly sure what it was. Whether it was a sense of propriety, or that her daughter was just a very good housekeeper, she had sent her to the class as soon as she heard of the opening in the nearby Village of Ryta, just ten miles east of Bratislava. Lizzie displayed an assertiveness that stood out among those humble working peasant people. She would argue with the adults, usually winning them over to her side. Her brothers would tease her, "Lizzie, you'll have many children someday, you can be the mother hen, then you can finally be in control."

In the evening after dinner, the Kuchen family would discuss events happening in their homeland of Czechoslovakia. Since 1843, revolutions began to occur throughout all of Europe. A group of Czechs demanded autonomous status for Bohemia within the Austrian Empire, rejecting an invitation to join with the Germans in the revolutionary Frankfurt Parliament. The Czechs instead turned their efforts toward their ethnic cousins of Eastern Europe and convoked a Pan Slavic Congress. The congress assembled in Prague in 1848 and passed a number of resolutions including one that demanded autonomy for all historic crownlands within the Hapsburg Empire. For more than a decade following the revolt of 1848, the new Austrian Monarch, Franz Joseph, ruled over the restless national groups with an iron hand. The weakened monarchy in Vienna now sought to stabilize its relationship with the Hungarians, whose revolt in 1848 had nearly succeeded in overthrowing Austrian rule. Concessions seemed to appear, but, in the end the emperor decided on autonomy for Hungary only. The historic compromise of 1867 established the Dual Austro-Hungarian monarchy, placating the Hungarians, but no other nationalities. The Compromise of 1867 had given the Hungarians exclusive rule over the territories inhabited by Slovaks while Bohemian crownlands were ruled by Vienna.

The Czechs formed their party in 1870 and gradually attracted the support of farmers, shopkeepers, and artisans who preferred their liberal approach to the nationalist program over the more conservative programs of old Czechs. The economic development that had begun in the 18th century intensified and created an industrial boom, catapulting Bohemia and Moravia into front ranks of Hapsburg-ruled lands. Along with industrialization came an increasingly differentiated social structure. Slovaks, who were unwilling to assimilate, met with discrimination in education, business, and government service and Slovak political activists were persecuted.

Seeing that the future of family life as they knew it to be was changing, Lizzie was disheartened to know that her mother, father and brothers would continue to be slaves working for the future of another country and keeping very little for their own future. She knew that she had to continue to develop whatever resources she had to someday leave that beautiful country life. Ambivalently, she waited for a sign from God for the direction her life would go. Yet, she knew that God would only give her faith in herself to go forward into the unknown. She would dare to be the person she was intended to be and it would not be easy. But she knew that she had whatever it took to be successful, wherever it might be in the world.

Walking home from the train station that Friday afternoon, Lizzie could hardly contain herself as she reached the Hovanek house at the end of her street. Something deep inside her was sending messages to go forward, go after your goals. She was terrified to announce her decision to her family. In the past, they would announce any plans, troubles, or personal concerns in their lives. It was routine in the evening at dinner sitting around the supper table. Then a rowdy discussion might develop. Recently, her older brother wanted to make a bicycle, like one he had seen somewhere in a German magazine called a draisine, with a steering bar connected to the front wheel.

"But Papa, I only have to buy the supplies, I can put it together," he cajoled.

"These things go too fast, you'll hurt yourself." End of discussion, Papa had spoken law. Papa wasn't always dictatorial, he usually encouraged them, but for some reason he thought bicycles were too unsafe. Lizzie could sense there was some rule or example set for the rest of them with this one.

A prayer was always said for a resolution. Yesterday her father and brothers brought in the remains of their bountiful harvest. Cabbages, squash, potatoes were stored in the cellar, silos piled high with hay, and corncribs were stuffed with cobs for fodder for the animals to last all winter. Bowing their heads before the enormous platter of steaming cabbage and dumplings Mama had prepared, and anticipating the grace they usually recited, Papa broke into another prayer.

Assuming his humble manner of furrowing his aging, weather-beaten brow, the grey forested eyebrows knit imploringly.

His soft voice spoke, "Dear God, we thank you for your golden harvest; you have been good to us this summer, please don't let 'those assholes' take it away from us."

This withstanding fear remained throughout the winter, as farmers all over worried the State would come and take some or all of their harvest. Papa had various hiding places located all over their farmland. Lizzie was disgusted and discouraged with a country who would usurp the reapings of hard work of their own poor people.

Lizzie resumed her present day task of making the bed she and Zach shared, counseling herself for taking precious time to indulge in day dreaming about another time. Shaking the heavy eiderdown comforter over the length of the bed, once again her mind retreated to another day long ago.

Walking home from the train she had marveled at the late autumn colors shining in the sun, it seemed she was noticing some things for the first time, like how immaculately clean the houses on their street looked. Almost all had lace curtains with different colored window frames. Was this because she was leaving? Nearing her small dark wooden house, she heard her mother singing through the open screened kitchen door.

"Tancuj, tancuj, vykkrucaj, vykrucaj.len mu piecku nezrucaj, nezrucaj; dobra piecka na zimu, na zimu nema kazdy perinu, perinu".

"(Dance, dance, whirl, whirl. Just don't disturb, disturb my oven. A good oven in the winter, in the winter—not everyone has an eiderdown, eiderdown!)".

The folk song recounted a tale about a young man going off to war to fight for a distant ruler while his lover is left alone. The song encourages the singer's partner to dance, but cautions her not to disturb the oven on which people must sleep in order to stay warm—because not everyone has an eiderdown.

Small blessings were considered important in the old country. Lizzie thought about Alexander Kocsie riding up to the door on his bicycle. Alex, a local boy, delivered messages and packages, or an occasional chicken or baby pig being exchanged among distant neighbors. His latest joy was that he might be able to keep the bike and use it for his own pleasure after working all day.

"I'm now on my way to prosperity," he told Lizzie, as she ran out to get the precious parcel from Mrs. Shandor, who lived two miles away. "I guess everyone has their own idea of success," she muttered, when Mama met her at the door anxious to examine the contents of the brown paper wrappings.

She lifted the tissue paper inside gingerly, revealing the thin, worn, paraffin coated, flower petal pattern used since the nineteenth century for stenciling linens, quilts, coverlets and all the fine, decorative scarves in their home. The priceless flowerlet replica represented their village of Moila. The humble people treasured it as one of the symbols of their autonomy. The flower had grown in numerous flocks on the hillside before the coal mines on the other side of town became of their chief exports. The coal dust began to spread to the outer limits now, gradually choking the natural resources in its path. Mama especially wanted Lizzie to participate in drawing the Flowerlet design onto the white quilted cotton quilt they were sewing for her oldest brother's wedding bed. He would marry in the spring, and he and his bride would move into the modest home they had all helped build next door on a small plot of land.

Lizzie loved these moments with Mama. Mama's

enthusiasm sparked her. She could turn even the most burdensome tasks into fun. Grasping the reality of leaving her family and this town with their past harshly ruled regimes led by Prince Metternich and his police minister Sedlnicky through their police state. Her heart felt proud that the integrity of the people reigned supreme. The spirit was strongly symbolized through these folk motifs which inspired nationalist feelings. Because literacy was rare among the peasants, stories and music were not actually written down until the nineteenth century. Czech music had not been as completely extinguished during the preceding "darkness" as the other arts and it achieved unprecedented heights with the emergence of the brilliant compositions of Bedrich Smetana, Antonin Dvorak and Zdenek Fibich. Dance steps, embroidery and sewing patterns and architectural plans were all transmitted orally by demonstration or emulation. Regions, and often, villages developed their own characteristic styles according to the tastes of their inhabitants and the nature of available materials.

The next morning Lizzie had awoke at dawn. She strolled through the woods to attend mass at the old stone church of St. Methodius Church where Father Hunse would celebrate the greater honor and glory of God. "Hospodine. pomiluj ny" (God Have Mercy Upon Us), were the songs and hymns of the Hussites which dated back to the Bohemian Reformation. They sang loud at the end of mass, believing that singing brought beautiful praises to God. Religion reflected all the unrest in their country, who would be on their side if God was not. He was their friend and leader.

As a young child, Lizzie ran dirty-faced into this church, genuflecting and a quick "I love you Jesus" was all she had time for. Father Hunse, with his dark haired head bending down to listen intently, had power in the community.

The people trusted him implicitly, following his advice about their personal problems. Lizzie thought if she would be in the religious life, she would like to be the pastor in a small village like Moila. But, the Church put only men into those positions. It seemed to be a sort of select league of the men of God—one had to be born a prestigious male to qualify. Deep inside she felt envious toward the piousness of the leaders of the church. Their isolation from women and children must surely make them vulnerable at times, and yet they controlled people's lives. The Holy Spirit seemed to shine on these priests—surely they must possess some unique gift. They were God's special people.

She looked at the altar, the sacristy and closed her eyes. Then she promised God if He would help her make her entry into her profession she would counsel her first born son to be one of his own. If she could not, as a woman, go forth to be in this wonderful position to bring God to the people, then those ahead of her would. A woman's life was a limited one: She was only a service unit of society. Her choices were only small ones, like which meal to serve her family that day, or, as in religion, to know, love and serve God. But she could not be in the administration of the church or sacraments.

She knew many good women, even more spiritual than men, who never sinned and always did good deeds throughout their entire life. Why couldn't they take their place beside the men in clerical positions? She seldom questioned her faith, but she didn't completely understand the process by which it was transmitted—through the church, to the people.

Chapter 2 The Skinny Girl

Their giggles echoed through the alley as they wrapped the braunswieger on rye and oatmeal cookies in waxed paper for Pop's lunch.

"Dell, you just have to meet this new man Pop hired to sell cars, he's the cat's meow," Mary said, pulling a brown bag from the cupboard. "What a good lookin' guy. A college boy, with a good future."

Dell began to wonder what Mary thought might be a "good lookin' guy," when Their Mother, Theresa, hustled into the room.

"Now, Pop is waiting for his lunch, you girls get going with that. Oh, maybe I should have made it myself," she mumbled, whisking them out of the door toward the automobile sales garage their father owned and operated next to their home.

But Dell wasn't interested in teaming up with any man, not yet, anyway. She'd <u>just</u> found a dream job as stenographer for the head of the Marketing Division at the new Envelope Company. Graduating third in her class at Valley Night School, she thought that might eventually land her the prized spot of secretary to the President.

By her own standards, Della Elona Gesner knew she was nothing to look at. Being a skinny girl, even her best dresses restlessly looked for a curve somewhere to hang on to. In this age of the "flapper," most of the women she knew had good bosoms and figures revealing voluptuous curves, especially her sister Mary. She would laugh at her older sister's thin presence, as if she thought Dell would eventually "fill-out." Even though styles were rapidly changing toward the leaner look, Dell still hadn't gone beyond the emaciated stage. Lately, she'd begun to emulate the clingy fashions of the sophisticated women she worked with, attempting to cultivate the stylish sheik look that was vogue. She'd spent yesterday after work getting her hair styled into a sleek new bobbed wave.

It wasn't just her looks that bothered her. Never knowing quite what to say could be humiliating. When she did attempt to start a conversation, it would always come out sounding awkward. Most of the time she did what Mom said.

"Just smile, let the other person talk. Be interested." This worked well, except when it was her turn to chime in. Today, when she and Mary met this salesman, she would follow Mom's advice.

They walked into the enormous automobile display room, heels clicking against the smoothly-painted cement floor where four different brand new model Chryslers were parked diagonally. Pop and a customer were examining the undercoating on a yellow coupe. They put his lunch and a large glass jar of coffee on his desk inside his office.

"C'mon Dell, there he is over there," Mary whispered.

Dell's new dark waves clung alongside delicately boned cheeks, as her bright enthusiastic eyes looked into Johnny's for the first time.

"Dell, this is Johnny Albred," Mary said with an ease Dell envied.

"Hi," they synchronized, their eyes meeting on a twinkle and a promise.

Dell's stomach leapt with excitement gazing at this interesting man with sandy hair and apple rosy cheeks. Bursting with joy, she thought about how he would be working right across the street from her house all summer long.

"What's say we take a test ride 'round the block in that new blue convertible roadster just in today," he said.

Dell loved his "take charge" attitude. No wonder he was a good salesman, she thought, bon vivant, a man of the world. Sure, she had a few boyfriends coming to the house from time to time, but Johnny did seem different. He even dressed differently, wearing the most unusual combination of clothes: striped pants with a checkered shirt.

At Johnny's suggestion, they all piled into the automobile. Heading swiftly over to the new cobblestone highway, Johnny looked over and smiled now and then at Dell sitting close to the door staring straight ahead. Highway construction had become a new major industry in 1924 with war surplus trucks bringing modern methods and materials. Engineers already knew how to use concrete and asphalt-bound macadam to heighten highway resistance to wheels and weather. But so far they had been mostly confined to larger towns and cities.

Johnny talked most of the time.

"Now, look at that guy, he's a hazard, he has no idea how to keep to the right side of the road. The state is going to have to begin regulating these roads. It's going to get dangerous out here."

Most people's lack of driving experience was obvious, since no one had been driving more than a few years. Dell was fascinated and enraptured by this smooth-talking young man who seemed to be just a few years older than herself. Where had he acquired all this worldly knowledge? Later, as they said goodbye, she felt short changed, as if she was walking out in the middle of a double feature movie at the Rivoli Theatre.

After a couple of weeks, Dell sat at her desk that

faced a big window which looked out on to the parking lot. Transcribing shorthand all day got very tiring, and her mind began to wonder for a moment. Men were stacking spare parts against a building, and on the other side was an automobile, exactly like the kind they had taken a ride in on that unforgettable day when she first met Johnny. Why hadn't he attempted to take her out since then, on a real date? Just the two of them. She wanted to get to know him. Dell knew he was a student, but didn't know his field of study. Maybe she didn't really appeal to him. What would a handsome, outgoing guy like him want with a scrawny thing like her, anyway? Yesterday, coming home after work she'd seen them. Johnny and those Barnacle twins, Bea and Betty, talking and laughing together. He'd waved to her nonchalantly as she walked by. They were having such a good time together. They were of the full-bodied variety, with platinum hair, Mae West doubles. Why were they always stopping by to look at one auto or another at the garage? Dell knew they didn't really have the money to buy one. They just wanted to flirt with Johnny. She wondered if he ever saw them any place away from the garage.

Could she have been wrong thinking he'd been, at least initially, attracted to her? She was angry at herself that she was becoming so absorbed in him. Last week she was excited about her new job and now this meeting had complicated her life. After all she was earning 50 dollars a week. Thinking about how she was now on Easy Street, the thought of her and Johnny as a couple passed for the time being. Anyway, it was only July. She still had until the end of summer to see him at Pop's garage before he went back to college. They would see each other often there.

Late summer sunlight spilled through the hotel window, radiating Johnny's room like a silent trumpet beginning a new day filled with monumental decision. Time and events of the past two months had chiseled away at all the in-place impeccable objectives, changing and twisting the mold forcing him to begin to change his entire life. He couldn't believe it was already the end of August. Today he was returning to school for another fall semester. Scratching his head, the nagging problem that lurked in the background ever since that evening he'd worked late. That damn John Kelsey had insisted on a price breakdown on the new '25 Chryslers coming out, he thought angrily. He'd been burning the midnight oil when she appeared in a dark dotted swiss dress carrying a tray with sandwiches and milk.

"Here, Johnny, you must be starved," she said shyly.

"Oh, thanks Dell. How about keeping me some company out here, I'll be finished in a minute."

She'd sat nibbling a cookie for another half hour until he had his tabulation finished.

"I wouldn't spend the time, but this guy is a sure sell," he said rolling down his sleeves. The radio was playing and Johnny began to whistle to the tune.

"I like that song," Dell started, then she began to sing the words softly.

Johnny sat down on the old leather divan beside her. He could feel the warmth of her skin through the thin material of her dress. A brilliant rush of excitement overtook him, as he gently held her face in his hands pulling her to him. Her lips were soft and inviting. Her eyelids were closed, then she broke away somewhat frightened.

"I have to get up for <u>work</u> tomorrow. I'll see you afterward."

And with that she left him staring after her freely flowing dress.

Why did this thorn have to be there among all the other special moments he and Dell had had the last couple of months. The freshness of her whole personality. When she entered the room it was as if a huge bouquet of flowers had sprouted. The walks and picnics they'd been on, saying nothing, but laughing at anything. Maybe a squirrel would flee across the street as they walked. This would be provocation for a giggle. Johnny could be himself with Dell. She didn't want to be entertained like some of the other women he'd met. He wondered if she was from the same planet as he. Life had taken on a new meaning for him. He found himself whistling often these days. Even his mother had remarked, "Hey, Johnny, are you that happy to be going back to school? Well that's good. We need a new Assistant Pastor at St. Helen's."

The day of reckoning had to come. He knew it had to come sometime he thought. Johnny knew he had to account for his previous actions in some way, to sort out his life once and for all. None of these new feelings would just go away. He had been vulnerable. He was wrong going against the grain of all the training and conditioning he had received at the seminary. Why had she caught his attention so dramatically? What factor was it that had stirred this excitement within his gut that he could not identify? He'd met many women, showing them cars, catching their flowery scent as they stretched long, limbering legs under the dashboard. But outward expressions of feminine wiles were purely cosmetic, all his classmates getting ready to go into the priesthood knew that.

"Don't get too close, you might catch some emotional affliction," they warned.

The Prelates implied this in almost every lecture, in their warnings about getting too involved with your parishioners. He had read his breviary every morning, noon and evening to guard against the invasion of too much worldly influence. Perhaps God wanted him to open up his mind.

Maybe he was meant to go in a different direction. He never even knew Pop had a daughter when he took this job. Maybe the whole thing was providential.

The cool hard tile of the bathroom floor felt good against the bottom of his hot feet, as he reached for the brass knob to turn on the hot water spigot full force. What was so different about Dell? He soaped his night growth of beard generously. Holding his face just so to the light, he took aim with his razor, making quick, nervous, strides through the stubble. Yeah, Dell was not like any other woman he knew. There was this untouchable naiveté, which put her on a different level than the ordinary woman. She had an unapproachable quality. Maybe it was those standards, choosing not to accept anything for face value. Trying to understand what was inside of a person, she took the time to think things through in these fast crazy days when so much was happening. She certainly didn't have outstanding looks. Walking with an assuming air, she always seemed to have been there before a couple of times, even though he knew she was unsure inside. She listened much more than she spoke, yeah, that must be it, listening, showing concern, compassion, that sincere understanding of a situation or a problem.

Some of the other women in town, like the Barnacle twins, were different. They coined the market on sensual looks but beauty was only on the surface. He wondered where they would be without bleached hair. They just didn't get to him and he was thankful for the immunity. But, they were attractive and had class, something to look for in a woman. Commonality, that's what it was called! The common denominator—it was what made women, women. Most men just liked to look and sometimes touch, but definitely not him, not with the course he was on, anyway. That is until this summer. He had practiced looking at such diversions and letting them quickly pass. God, he thought, it would never come to this kind of decision making.

He wasn't a virgin. He had plenty of opportunities to make that stand true. Living away from home, in prep school at St. Vincent's for ten years could ruin a guy's soul. The "fellahs" there made sure they all got laid at one time or another. Nothing serious, just a one-nighter. He'd never forget the first time for him, he must have just turned sixteen. Edna was her name and she was more than a consenting adult, she was the initiator. He and Jack and Al all went out for beers that night. Edna and her friend, Fran were at the next table. They were older, divorced and had obviously been around. Johnny could tell by the way those dames were amused at all the vulgar language and the goo-goo eyes they made back and forth, that they'd be an easy lay.

At the mere hint, they all squeezed into Edna's jalopy headed for who knows where. She had this red hair, all over her body, he found out later. It looked like bright lights were on all over the place. He had never seen so much red hair. No sooner had they gone into her apartment—a maze of boxes full of sample foundations for women's bodies—than she ran him into the bedroom for testing, saying, "Now, let's see what ya got down there, Buster?"

Apparently, she was peddling these modern garments all over the eastern states and, somehow he became her new sample nightwork foundation for the night. If she could have fitted him for a corset or brassiere later, she would have been happy. This was all clinical, experimental, no passion, no romance much less emotional upheaval of any kind. In a way he was relieved. This confirmed what sex was all about. It was all so easy. Get it up, put it in, and get it off. It was all part of God's biological plan for men. Just walk away later, relieved, no conscience-wringing entanglements. He wasn't sure whether women were included in this scheme of things. He always thought their primary purpose was to have babies, to procreate. He wasn't sure whether they were meant to enjoy the same sexual privileges as men. They were part of the world, but not his future. His love was a deep spiritual love for God. Sure Mom initiated the whole thing. But he wanted it too, didn't he? In the seminary preparation program they learned that God was of the Divine world and people were part of the secular world they would interact with. Two divided entities. Putting it into perspective, it was all clean cut. Having to choose between God and an earthly being is enormously difficult. It was like being torn between two different conflicting loyalties, yankin' your heart in two directions and still going on one crooked path toward God.

Last spring he was told by the Dean that he would enter the seminary the following year. The first thing they were officially told was to "steer clear of girls and women before going home for summer vacation." Despite that, this was the first summer he truly had enjoyed. He looked forward to seeing Dell every day as she walked in smiling as she was always did. She usually came home at five, the time his regular customers starting stopping in after work. Lately he had begun greet her with a kiss. He couldn't hold back, they were both jubilant to see each other. It was like going to morning mass and hearing the angels sing. But, these cherubs were singing other kinds of praises, the kind a man feels for a woman, uplifting the spirits of love. Until that point, he knew how it felt to love God, his mother, father, family, but, this all-consuming craving in the pit of his stomach was telling him there was another kind of love out there, the love of a man for a woman, and vice versa. Although he'd been careful not to be completely alone with her this summer, it was too much of a temptation and the inevitable happened.

The one most important thing he learned in prep school was how to examine his conscience. Now there was conflict. He was lusting, mentally committing adultery day in and day out.

He was feeling the effects of emotional upheaval, not something normal in the course of his nicely laid out life. Sure, he enjoyed being among people especially when he was selling cars. He knew he was good at it, reaching out to people in that way. Pop believed in his business sense, in fact, he left him totally on his own in the garage. He'd trusted him to follow the sale of the car from the beginning to the close of the deal. It was all mostly cash up front.

Aside from selling cars, the only other real life he knew was at school. Though the hotel was a prosperous business, Mom kept him out of there, fulfilling some plan of having her oldest son become a priest since the day he was born. It was almost as if he were born wearing a chasuble, the outer colored vestment priests put on over the rest of their vestments. He'd always thought that a vocation came by way of a special messenger of God, as in most of the stories of the saints lives. St. Francis of Assisi received the stigmata as a sign. And the Angel Gabriel appeared to the Blessed Mary at her annunciation, others had visions. Saints Augustine and Thomas Aquinas were lifetime students of the church. Where would we be without their teachings? Many were politicians, especially the apostles.

When he had neared his fourteenth birthday, the talk around the Albred Hotel became clearer, even Zach mentioned it openly among the patrons, as he stood behind the long, dark mahogany bar.

"Well, John will be soon be going to preparatory school to begin to learn about the priesthood." This proclamation was announced as if it's now time to take out the newspapers, they're piling up. But, of course, Zach's tone of voice had a downward kind of sound. It was as if he was saying something he felt doubtful about. He had known from a very early age, that Lizzie had planned this for him, but was not sure how the resolution would be carried out. Then, when he was twelve, Father O'Flaherty sat down and talked to him at a small table at the back of the hotel restaurant. It seemed to be a clandestine meeting as he bent very close to Johnny, his iridescent, red Irish-skinned neck straining over his tight white collar.

"Now, Juhnny, me boy, yer mum tells me the day is fast approachin' for yer schoolin' to begin. Aye 'n ye musn't be afeared, the good bruthers'll take care o' ye."

He seems like he's already 40 sheets to the wind, Johnny thought, inhaling the strong alcoholic vapor on his breath, and it's only about four o'clock in the afternoon. He'd grown up watching men stagger out of the bar very early in the afternoon even though prohibition was in full swing.

"Johnny, the trunk of the car is all emptied out." He could hear his mother's voice traveling down the hall jerking him back to the present day. He hurried across the room to shut the door. He did not want her coming into his room abruptly, as she usually did.

"Okay, Ma, thanks," he shouted back against the dark wood, his hand still clasping the knob. Besides, his face just might reveal some inward expression he didn't want to discuss with anyone just now. He finished dressing and grabbed two large suitcases.

It was September again, another new year of school beginning, as he drove through the historic roads of Ligonier. Grey cement had converted to slightly golding trees along solid green countryside miles ago, when his foot had tramped heavily on the clutch, throwing the gear shift into third on their Chrysler Imperial. Lizzie had allowed him to bring his suitcases to the car—he'd bring the car back over Labor day weekend, taking the train back again.

Growing up, Johnny knew Lizzie was no ordinary mother. She did very little mothering. There wasn't much affection in their hotel-household atmosphere. Lizzie never held or hugged any of them as they were growing up. There was never time, she was too busy. Johnny wondered how she'd even taken time to give birth to any of them. Remembering when he was younger, living in Scranton, it seemed that life was less hectic then, before they bought the hotel. Philip and Agatha were, more or less, left to encounter life on their own. No wonder they were always in trouble. He'd taken care of them most of the time, but it was getting pretty tough to keep up with their antics. He wished his Mom would pay attention to them more often, become a real person, at least in their presence. He never saw her hair down. She always had it tied in a tight knot at the top of her head. It was pure white and very straight, just like the large apron she wore.

Arriving on campus long before vespers, Johnny thought he would take a moment before unloading his luggage to make a visit to the church. Entering the huge vestibule of St. Benedict's Cathedral, he plunged two middle fingers into the immense marble holy water fount, genuflected and blessed himself, making the sign of the cross. Knowing there would be monks and priests praying their breviary, he walked softly down the narrow side steps of the winding wrought-iron staircase to the chapels and grottos beneath the towering cathedral.

In the near darkness, he found a short pew and sat down to reflect in the hollow stone tunnel. Bowing his chin down against his clasped fingers, he stared out at a reflective design cast by millions of tiny red flickering votive candles. He thought about his mother and how they had gone to mass every morning as he was growing up. She had always held priests in high esteem, thinking they were on the same level as the President of the United States. They were an authority in the town and their power was never questioned. When Father O'Flaherty walked into the hotel, it seemed as if the

Pope himself had arrived; Lizzie would roll out the red carpet—anything he desired in the hotel was his. He also would win any argument that may have ensued at the bar, becoming moral judge and jury over any of the heated discussions. One provocative issue was which sins were mortal and which were venial. Sometimes, Johnny would notice people come in the swinging door only to leave again upon seeing Father officiating there. They would turn around, as if through a revolving door, before he could admonish them for not attending church regularly.

He'd never forget the first time they drove out to the countryside to this school, in Latrobe, about fifty miles from home in rural eastern Pennsylvania. It was a complete change from all the commotion of the city where he'd grown up. His mother fixed her bright, suspicious eyes on him.

"John, you will make a wonderful priest," she said, imploring him to defy her authority, as she so often did to her subjects. He didn't think there were any other options in life. St. Vincent's was a huge preparatory school and college, run by the Benedictine Fathers. They operated independently, doing their own farming, with livestock, including a sauerkraut tower. The Benedictines took care of them. They were "the boys." The upperclassmen made fun of them and worked hard at creating torture for them, the louses, taking their beds apart when they were out of the building, or dumping garbage in front of their dorm room. This happened about an hour before curfew, so by the time they'd cleaned it up they were too tired to remake their beds and usually ended up sleeping on the wooden floor. Sliding down the long wooden banisters was a practice until the upperclassmen coated them with some black sticky stuff. He thought it was tar. Too bad he was late for class that morning and couldn't change his knickers—they were his best ones. He'd gotten thirty demerits that day, causing him to loose many privileges, like being able to leave the campus to see the girls at St. Joseph Academy near by.

Turning fifteen, he went out for the football team. He was a natural. Father Edmonds, the coach told him he was one of the best receivers the Bears ever had, and that he had great plans for him. He even made the local newspapers. That's when Mom saw that he was doing other things up there beside learning to be a priest. According to her, he was supposed to sit in a darkened room and pray all day. Sure enough, within a few days, she was up there talking to the Dean about transferring him to another school unless he made sure Johnny was off the team. What could he do? She was bound and determined to see him ordained according to her schedule. For the most part, he wanted to go along with her plan for him, but he began to visualize it looking like a lonely kind of life, especially at the age of eighteen. It was then that he was told that he had to learn to detach himself from family ties before entering the seminary, having limited contact with the outside world, leaving worldly things behind. This was difficult for him because of his strong need to be with people.

But now he was approaching an age where he absolutely had to decide which direction his life was going. Any decision would cause a lot of problems, especially for his mother.

He knew he couldn't be celibate, affection would be a nice feature in his life. Existence would be a big empty space without the close warmth of another human being there. Age fourteen was not the time to decide to be celibate anyway. He knew that he had a passionate love for God, since he learned to love him first. But there was another life out there, and he had to find it. He loved Dell. They might even have children. He would be a better father than a priest. He did not believe that everyone who was ordained into the priesthood were called to celibacy. This whole religious cycle would work if married men could be priests. This will never change my love for God, he thought, entering the chapel and staring up at the radiantly domed ceiling. He knelt and prayed for a better understanding of what God wanted from him.

Chapter 3 Implacable

Lizzie was not sure exactly when she decided to come to America. It might have been immediately after finishing cooking school, or when she and her childhood friend, Annie, were walking home from church talking about their chances for working at the Grand Hotel of Bratislava.

"Madame knows the manager, she could recommend us as salad girls or to assist the kitchen inventory staff," Lizzie said exploringly.

"Yes, we have to try for something, even if it is just a cleanup person. But how can we be as good as the big city people who have lived and worked there all their lives?" Annie spoke with downcast eyes.

As the day grew nearer to when they would get their certificate, Lizzie began to think about the future. Her brothers began to make comments at supper about match-making.

"Lizzie, have you seen the handsome young clerk at the railway station in Ryka? I hear he's single and looking for a good wife, and what a fine position he has with the railroad."

Lizzie caught the cynicism twinkling in the eyes of her father belying any credibility she might have for a future beside the one of being someone's wife. They will never understand, she thought. A woman does not always find her goal in life with a man. His comment was more than she could bear. This was one trap she would guard against. She had spent too many hours working toward her career to squander it away as some man's servant. She knew too many of her friends who were living their lives attending to a husband in a marriage planned by their parents. And, though she knew that her parents probably wouldn't do this, she was not sure they wouldn't fall prey to leading her into the position of being "safe" with someone who had a fine position to support them both comfortably.

Lizzie tossed and turned under her warm perinu that cold winter night with thoughts leading to logical escape routes to opportunity. Where would her beginning point begin? A full moon shone through the window onto her flannel nightgown, as she slid out of bed to kneel on the rag braid rug. The cold chill blew against her legs from the bare cold wood floor.

"Dear Lord, please direct my thoughts, please show me the route to take toward new beginnings."

She prayed. Jumping up, she tripped over a small school book in her path. Glancing at the cover depicting a man and woman holding a bushel of fruit from the state of California set her heart beating wildly. This was a book about America that she held in her hand. It was a sign from God. She would find her future in America.

Every day she would put new information she was collecting about America in a small cardboard box. She talked to Madame Petrovka about some references at hotels there and possibly a place to stay. In 1880 the idea of coming to America was not very popular in her town and, even though they had only heard about the revolutions in nearby countries, the threat of the oncoming revolution by yet another country could suddenly uproot the temporary peace of the village. Then her hopes and dreams would have no possibility. Lizzie was motivated by an ambition to command her own kitchen staff and turn out masterful culinary wonders.

An independent mind in social situations was not new to Lizzie, people had always followed her example and ideas. After having seen a horse beaten while overburdened with a heavy load she had led a local campaign a few years ago for the farmers to treat farm animals more humanely. To perpetuate this idea, she coaxed her brother to walk around the farms with her taking notice of living conditions in barns and stables. At first, farmers resented the young woman entering their private domain, but eventually she gained the trust of the townspeople and they began to watch for inhumane treatment. It was just her way of getting involved in an injustice. Furthermore, she had the courage to strike an awareness.

Madame Petrovka's friend, Michael, had told her about a small group of people who would be leaving for America at the beginning of September, just a few days after her eighteenth birthday. The little group gathered to talk about the pending trip. Among them were three professional people: a physics teacher, medical doctor and a musician. The cost was twenty dollars in American money. Lizzie was glad that she had put away a small amount the last two years from the money that Papa had given her from selling vegetables in Ryka, although she knew it would not be enough to carry her through once she arrived at her new home. Her stomach began to flutter with excitement at the prospect of opportunity. Just how it would present itself, she was not ready to speculate, but she folded and refolded the slips of paper that Madame had given to her with the names and addresses of distinguished hotel proprietors in three large cities: New York, Philadelphia, and Boston.

"We can find a room together and work side by side," Annie implored anxiously.

But Lizzie tried to discourage her by saying, "You will

will miss your family. It may be difficult. You have always had sick spells, who will take care of you?"

She was a delicately boned young woman predisposed to colds and illness and did not seem to possess the stamina required for the long voyage. But Annie had remained firm in her resolution to be Lizzie's traveling companion.

"There is no place for me here. Mama and Papa will grow old and then what kind of a life will I have? I want to see America, I want to be with you."

Lizzie was overwhelmed by the trust that her friend had shown in her, and felt comforted by the fact that she would not be alone.

The leader of their travel group, Mr. Kovacik, encouraged them to travel light carrying only small personal valuables with them. Lizzie gathered together a white gilded prayer book from her first Holy Communion and a tiny red silk pin cushion Mama had sewn for her sixteenth birthday. She was not sure where Mama had purchased the precious material tufted into the delicate shape of their village flower and fringed with two rows of crocheted love knots. Mama had probably bartered in the market place with either baked goods, fruit or vegetables for the small precious scrap of material and other goods needed for the family. She could see Mama arguing with the vendors, "No, they're worth much more, and I'm not leaving till I get my price." She would get her price in the end, her dark brown eyes concentrating on her victim to achieve her ultimate goal. A tear filled Lizzie's eye as she thought of the devotion and goodness of Mama and how she would miss her.

Suggesting that they dress in layers to prevent them from packing a lot of unnecessary clothes made most of the travelers laugh, since most had only one change of clothes:

one for every day and another for church on Sundays. Kovacik brought their passports back and talked about the dangers of separating from each other while on the long, two and one half week voyage at sea. He was a merchant who lived in Trieste. His travel took him back and forth many times looking for valuable treasures which ranged from jewelry to furniture and decorative carriages for export to America and other countries. Usually his cargo was full. They were lucky there was room for passengers on this particular trip.

Mama held a small gathering for Lizzie. All the neighbors wished her Godspeed, each giving some token for her new life in America. She received numerous koruna and crowns, which would come in handy later in her journey. These good people had watched her grow up into the determined young woman that she'd become. Many expressing confidence in her future success.

"You will make us very proud, Lizzie, going out into the world," shouted Mrs. Masaryk, who had once wanted to leave the village, but had been firmly held in tow by elderly parents and forced to marry an older man and friend of her father's.

Why did these entrapments occur so often to women, when men could travel for miles to find their ultimate goals? Lizzie had been adamant about her choice to go forward into the world with her talent, but if it wasn't for strength of character and strong faith in God, she would have been shepherded into a completely different life. There were many examples of this within the families on the street where she lived all of her life. There was Mr. Capek, who was opposed to her going alone, even though she would be accompanied by six of her compatriots. He talked with her father almost daily about the dangers she would face, "a young woman out there in the world alone will only find trouble." She worried that these intimations would force her father to dissuade her from leaving them in good stead. He could never discourage her, not when she was at this crucial point in her life. Sending her away without his blessing would injure the confidence that she needed to overcome all of the obstacles which would present themselves. As the day approached Papa seemed to be visibly nervous.

"There will be no one there for you when you need them, Elizabeth. What will happen when you are sick?"

"Papa, haven't I always shown that I can take care of myself? There is a big world out there, and I have something to offer. If I find that my cooking skills are not comparable to what is expected, I will come back. You know God is always with me."

In his heart he knew she had more strength than all of them to persevere with her ambition.

Lizzie's relationship with her father was a respectful one—she looked up to him as the head of their household. But, she did not agree with his attitude toward her mother and herself, always putting the women last even though they carried their load of the work equally. In arguments her father always had to have the last word, never admitting to being wrong. In this sense her objectives had to be established. It was the only way to show herself as a woman who could succeed in a man's world. She knew her ambition to succeed was superior to many young men her age, but she was different. She had a plan to achieve her goal.

Large intricate, laced snowflakes fell on her nose and eyelashes melting as they hit the warmth of her skin. It was the first cold day of November, All Souls Day. Lizzie clutched the small cotton purse pinned inside the black wool sweater Mama had knitted for her last year. The koruna inside purse formed an awkward lump next to her side, reminding her to guard it carefully since it could never be replaced if lost on the journey. The sun shone on the small group gathering to walk to the Ryka train station. They would purchase their train tickets for Bratislava / Vienna and get their steamer ticket in Vienna to board at the port of Trieste, Yugoslavia for New York Harbor.

Lizzie stepped up to the window and peered through the bars at the clerk there. Her brother was right, this was a handsome and likable young man. She knew he would find a nice wife who would clean his house and have his children. A green visor covered a mop of straight blond hair, grey sincere eyes shined toward hers expressing a desire to get to know her better. Too bad, she thought, we might have become friends. But I'm on my way to more exciting things. And, though on the precipice of one of the most principal events of her life, she felt deep sorrow leaving her family and the peasant's way of life, the only life she had ever known. One part of her wished she could have found a way to satisfy her aspirations here in the village. But the other part of her nature urged her to go forward into the world arena to compete with the foremost culinary chefs. This thought motivated her. She had to sacrifice some of her sentimentalities to do this. She would be grateful to her family and humble beginnings forever for endowing her with the fortitude manifested within her to get to this point.

She and Annie ran to get a seat in the first car of the train which expended some of her tense energy. Sharing the seat with three others didn't bother her as she crouched up to the window waving to friends and family who had walked with them to the station.

"I will write as soon as I'm able, God bless you, take care of yourself, I'll send a ticket to you as soon as I can," filled the train.

Emotional sobs flowed as steam poured forth signaling

the wheels to start down the track toward the Little Carpathian Mountain pass and on to Vienna. Continuing to stare out the window, Lizzie caught the last glimpse of Mama's brown babushka as they passed the corner of the station. Then a chilling thought occurred to her that she may never see them ever again. Dear God, she thought, please keep my family safe and free from harm. Her mind wandered to the location where her journey would finally end. What would she actually find there? She knew that the streets were not paved in gold in America as so many had said. Madame Petrovka had attested to this.

"Don't be disillusioned into thinking that these opportunities will come to you on a silver platter. No, you will all have to work from the bottom up. You may have to do the lowliest work first such as washing dishes, peeling potatoes, mopping the floor—all of the basic jobs in a kitchen. But if you show the desire, a good attitude to learn their system, before you know it you will climb to the top of the ladder and you will be put in charge!"

Lizzie never forgot how her eyes had glistened with enthusiasm speaking those words on their last day of school. Madame had worked with the best, she knew how the system operated and Lizzie trusted her judgment implicitly.

But what if she failed and could not pass the test in America? She struggled to keep her outlook positive. She would approach it one step at a time. Madame had contacted some people for them to meet—they would go to Philadelphia first. The Erie Railroad traveled out of New York to Philadelphia. What odd sounding names, Schenectady and Niagara. She had even seen a city by the name of Hoboken which made her laugh. Some of these cities were named for American Indians: Schenectady meant "End of trail" because it lay at the meeting point of Indian trails from the north, south and east. In their small school where Herr Becker taught them reading, she had learned some of the history of America. The Indians were the first to live there, but were forced to leave so that the English Colonists could settle on their lands. She wondered if the same thing would happen to them. If America was home to the free and the brave, how could they have fought so hard to get rid of the first inhabitants of the land?

The librarian at the University of Bratislava had given her current American magazines to read and polish up her slow, broken English. She had learned several cooking terms, "brown the meat," "a pinch of salt," "stir the batter to a smooth consistency" and "flour the board." She would greet everyone with a smile of confidence, saying "Good Morning" or "Good Day." If she watched the cook very closely she would understand immediately what process was going on. It would not be difficult. She would concentrate on the task at hand and not let a lack of confidence distract her. At least, until she watched the kitchen organization at work. Lizzie knew how to get along with people. It was easy for her to get them to like her. She showed an interest in them instantly and wasn't that what everyone wanted, generally, to be noticed and liked? But this was not what she, herself, required. She wanted respect for bringing her craft across the ocean from Czechoslovakia, the wonderful country that had so much to offer the world. She was their emissary, carrying with her an undisclosed culinary cache of treasures and delights of the Czech-Hungarian kitchen, dishes like Veal Steak Paprikas' and Gulyas' of every variety, which she would shower on the American people.

White Star Oceanic Steamship was written clearly on the side. Vocalizing the vowel sounds W h i t e and

O c e a n i c out loud, the group of six walked slowly to their small cabins. Minuscule but clean, she thought squinting through the tiny porthole. This would be her view for the long duration of the sea voyage, an endless vista of water for two weeks, or longer, depending on the weather. She had never seen the ocean before that day, this vast body of water going between all bodies of land. Reaching out to cities where millions of different people lived, like America, where all different kind of people lived all together on one continent. Kovacik had talked to them about all the different nationalities that lived together in just one city. Madame Petrovka was Hungarian and Carl Nieberding, a German boy, was in her class in cooking school. And though their country was ruled by other countries for many years, each nationality continued to live separate in their own little towns. She had never seen an African. How would she, as a Czechoslovakian, be received by the American people. She had heard that they were enterprising. They had many modern inventions there which would make them an industrialized nation. Her stomach was sore and ached with excitement. She would do everything she could to become one of them.

The dark cold waters moved the vessel slowly as the monotony of one day melded into another. Sunday became Tuesday, and Tuesday became Thursday before Lizzie realized she was beginning to vegetate within the confines of the cabin. Most of the time, she and Annie would play games, matching pictures with the English words. That evening, as Annie closed her eyes to sleep, Lizzie went off to explore other areas of the large seagoing monster. Following the long grey corridors, she walked along speedily. Being a slim young woman, she hid in the small crevices lining the hallway if some custom official should appear out of nowhere. She made her way to the ship's kitchen in no time at all. Crouching slowly toward the white tile floor, she heard voices speaking in English, something about these "greenhorns and hunkies." The staff was not happy about having to prepare meals, if that's what they called them, for the foreigners.

"Who's there, hey?" the tall one shouted at her. A short fat man in a uniform which barely covered his body grabbed her by the arm.

"Hey, whadaya think yer doin' there, sister?" With all her fearlessness behind her, Lizzie cringed as they lunged at her, and, knowing these men had hostility toward her, added to her terror.

"Ya lousy greenhorn, why'r ya spyin' on us? Don' ya know we already got enough of yer likes in the states? We can't even feed them's we have."

Not knowing exactly what they said, their tortuous bearded faces were enough for her to realize the mistake she had made in going down there. Why were they so angry? Did all of the people in America feel this way about the immigrants? She managed to break free, running with fury back to her cell. She thought these small quarters she shared with Annie had become her prison, as she watched high lapping waves splashing at the porthole. Glancing at Annie, who lay sallow on her cot, she began to dread what was on the other side of this ocean. She had left her warm family and the people of her village for uncertainty. Trust yourself Lizzie, she reflected, trust yourself and trust God. With that she prayed herself to sleep. Thank God tomorrow would be a fresh new day, and she could begin a new account of the world.

Land. It looked beautiful. Tall buildings jutted out of the fog-born sky like fifty steeples grouped together in one setting. The only comparable structure Lizzie had ever seen was the Prazsky hrad, the Prague Castle. The women were instructed to go to the left and the men to the right as they walked disconcertedly down the boat's plank into another world. Bewildered stares of excitement or fear, whichever crossed their mind first, transcended their moment in time. Intolerable noises of fog horns, neighing horses, motors and loud voices of people forced their way into their senses as the pounding sights of commerce held them spellbound along their stride into a small inspection station. A rather nice, stout woman placed a huge tag around Lizzie's neck with the city of her destination, Philadelphia, written on it. She knew the word well from her studies, it was all she could recall, her mind was a blank at the moment. None of the places or people, besides those she had spent the last two and a half weeks with, were familiar. Her first contact with an American searching her body for some unknown illness was not that horrible.

"Elizabeth Kuchen, Slavic!"

The Immigration Officer shouted as if "Slavic" summed up the entire eastern European nation. Her autonomy had been left at home in her special little village. She had lost her identity here in this new nation. She was overwhelmed with sadness as she looked at her country people. Their eyes were downcast and the little suffering group seemed to be mourning the death of a loved one. It would be hard to find a life here. One step at a time, she told herself. She still had her abilities as marketable here as any other place, recalling her confidence forefront.

"Get the Erie B & O train ticket for Philadelphia, Pennsylvania," Kovacik instructed gathering them together at close of their journey to give them his address if they should need to call him or the immigration authorities.

Two women dressed in the fashions of the day walked in front of them wearing swirling pleated skirts with pouches of material above their backsides. She found out later it was called a bustle. The decade of the 1880's led into the "Gay

90's" with the spirit of the nation. Mark Twain called it "The Gilded Age" because of its showy wealth. Such a display of luxurious quality in clothes had never been seen by Lizzie. Her interest mounted. One of the women giggled as Lizzie caught herself staring uncontrollably. What must they think of her gawking at them in that way, peeking from the side of her babushka, her cotton stockings starting to bag and her look of a bonafide rag-a-muffin? She was fulfilling her role as the greenhorn in every sense of the word as the rugged cook on the steamer had said. Feeling humiliated at the entire predicament, she was certain there would be many similar ones to come.

Unbeknownst to Lizzie, her arrival couldn't have happened at a better time in American History. The Civil War had ended in 1865 and America was beginning industrialization in the northeast.

"Let Us Have Peace," Ulysses S. Grant would urge, as he accepted the Republican nomination for President in 1868. Young, enterprising people such as herself would begin to build and prosper in a growing America on the path to being a world-wide power.

An odd little vehicle called an omnibus dropped them off at the Baltimore and Ohio Railroad Station where they would board for Philadelphia. Clickety-clacking out of the station, the train reminded Lizzie once again of their glorious departure in the comforting little village, as the grim stillness of their arrival descended upon them. A robin flew ahead of them on to the platform and she and Annie witheringly picked up their sacks and walked up on to the splintered wooden step toward the station master. Grasping the crumpled list, "Walnut Street" rang from her lips nervously. Then a nice thing happened. The station master smiled at them both, "How can I help you, Miss?" his deep throaty voice entreated. Lizzie responded with a strained smile, and held out her hand displaying the list for him to see. "Welcome to our city." He said. Lizzie knew the German word "Welcommen." She tried to respond with thank you, but it came back "tank you," and she was embarrassed once again. But the man did not laugh, instead he reached out a kind hand guiding them to a carriage pulled by a beautiful mare and helped them up the step. That was a most comforting oasis in their difficult road of travel which Lizzie wished would go on and on.

Knocking on the first white door of The Philadelphia Hotel, Administration Offices, where their first reference from Madame, Mrs. Palmer worked, brought a negative nod from the man who glanced down at their note. They turned around instantly and made their way up Walnut Street and onto Broad Street toward what they thought would be prospective employment. The afternoon was wearing on and they began to worry that they would have no room for the night.

"We would be pleased to have you start tomorrow," said the proprietor, Mrs. Greenaway, who had received a letter earlier that week announcing their arrival by the distinguished Madame Petrovka.

Lizzie and Annie danced a polka that evening in their little stark room. A new resolution came over Lizzie, together with hope for her future life. She would scrub all the pots with a vengeance, clawing her way into a prime position. Mrs. Greenaway had laughed at their appearance, especially when she and Annie had stumbled over the oriental rug in front of her desk. Lizzie knew that they must have been a sight at their first interview in America. She had tried to pull her enthusiasm from within to impress Mrs. Greenaway with her hidden cultivation, as she maintained a professional aplomb.

"You will start at ten dollars a week, with room and board provided, however, you will have to take the smallest room."

She was not sure whether Annie would be hired or not. Later she met Annie in the scrub down room where they were directed to strip and scrub with strong soap and a brush before climbing the thickly red carpeted stairs which would soon lead to bare wood as they rose to the very top to their quarters. Lizzie found out that Annie had been hired as one of the maids. Annie had not acquired any special trades, however, she had worked for some of the wealthy land owners in Bratislava which had given her a certain amount of cultural refinement. Lizzie admired her for being able to convey this to Mrs. Greenaway and, although she would not receive the same amount of money as Lizzie, they could share a room and their daily bread at the hotel.

Leaving little time for leisure, the fourteen hour long days at the huge hotel became drudgeries for the two young immigrants. The rest of the hotel staff, mostly Irish immigrants, respected the eastern Europeans and admired them for coming alone to the continent with their aspirations. But the kitchen chief had her own ambition.

"Git them pots ashinin' girl, don't ya be dreamin' bout some better life here, ya got to earn yr' fare like the rest of us, y'r a long way from the cabbage patch now."

She listened to Clara's commands day after day, usually mixed with an insult or two about her homeland which she missed gravely. Late at night with sore, cracked hands and a back racked with pain, Lizzie would search impatiently through the dictionary pages for the words that Clara and others spoke so crudely in the kitchen. Trying to learn English, she found the words that she did not necessarily want to include in her repartee.

Finding their nationality church, St. Michael's, became a quest for Annie and Lizzie. They met a Czech woman there named Greta Polinchak who worked at a nearby hospital. Agreeing to go to six o'clock mass the next Sunday and stay for a get-together afterward worried them.

"Oh, why did we tell her we'd come?" Annie said in her soft little voice, "Clara will threaten us with termination."

"We said we'd come and we will," Lizzie answered. "We have to meet some of our own kind of people here. It'll be the only way we can make this country our home." But a tear formed in her eye, as she thought it would be many years before they could call this their home.

A local man and parishioner, Zachariah Albred frequented those get-togethers. Mostly helping with the refreshments, he would warm up to the strange new immigrants. Since he had been in America for two years, he knew the loneliness and discouragement they felt. Working in the coal mines in Wilkes-Barre had worsened the black-lung disease he had acquired in the crude mines of Pecs. Now he loved spending time at the greenhouse on the outskirts of town, having some time to spare in the off- seasons. Zach was a mild-mannered man. Since he grew up in the country in Hungary, he had to work at cultivating a gentlemanly refinement. Towering over six feet tall with a stocky build, patches of white hair had begun to appear among sandy strands as his forty-third birthday appeared.

All the newly-arrived women of Europe loved Zach and most of them had serious marriage plans for him, but he wasn't interested. He steered clear of any of those longings. Having turned into an avid planter/florist earning a modest living, he was happy with the basic things of life. He enjoyed Lizzie's pugnacious manner and questioned her about her future plans.

"I'm going to run a big hotel," she answered in a dialect very near his own. Since Hungarian rule of their country had brought language skills of many varieties to Eastern

Europe, including Hungarian, Austrian and German.

"This is quite an ambition for someone who is fresh off the boat. How do you expect to achieve this—are you a millionaire?"

Zach was beginning to get too inquisitive and Lizzie avoided eye contact with him after that day. She did not want to share her plans with anyone, especially this man. But Zach was attracted to the indifference she displayed and pursued her even more.

"Go over and see Maria Marsalek, she has been having trouble with her landlord, go cheer her up!" Lizzie directed him one day when he began to show her too much attention.

Annie laughed at her on the way home.

"Zachariah has some notions about you, Lizzie. He isn't a bad man, why don't you be nice to him?"

"He's just going to get in my way, and you know the way these men think," Lizzie retorted. "They don't think you can accomplish your goals if you're a woman and especially since I've just come over he will never realize that every obstacle is another incentive for me."

Annie looked intently at her friend. She was her reason for being here. What courage, She thought. Annie could not imagine what her life would be like without Lizzie. She was such a good, strong woman. But, Annie had not been feeling very well lately and she didn't know who to tell about her health problem. She was afraid to tell Lizzie, who never felt any weaknesses. Before she could contain herself it was out.

"I'm having very bad stomach pains, Liz, and I feel like I've got a fever."

"Here, hold on to me," Lizzie said supportively, as she pulled her arm through Annie's. She put Annie in her shabby little bed and went down to see Mrs. Greenaway in her office.

Annie was diagnosed as having cholera.

"She must have come in contact with the germ while cleaning one of the rooms. The body poisons have spread considerably," Lizzie overheard the Doctor announcing the ominous news.

With haste, the Doctor and Mrs. Greenaway had Annie moved into quarantine to an isolated room over a nearby carriage house behind the hotel. Heartbroken that her friend might die, Lizzie peeked in on her from the door, afraid that she would be infected with the dreaded disease. Garden tools, cleaning supplies and used bed frames from the hotel cluttered the sides of the room, as Lizzie watched her courageous friend lying in the railed bed weak with dehydration. Hanging on to her last life support, Annie opened her ashen eyes,

"I'm glad that I was able to come here with you, Lizzie. I know you'll be a success. You have so much to offer the world. Don't come any closer, I don't want us both to die."

The flame of a votive candle burned quietly. Kneeling alone in the dark hollowed church was the shadowy form of a young woman.

"Dear Lord, please bless Annie's soul and give me the strength to go on to find the life for me. I know that you have brought me this far for good reason. Help me to go forward to do it."

Her sobs brought the man, who had been quietly saying his rosary, forward to see who interceded with such zeal. Zach looked consolingly.

"I know that you feel bad about Annie's death, Lizzie, but she followed her life's road to the end the way she wanted it to be. That is more than many people are able to do. She wanted to come here and be with you. She lived her adventure to the end."

Lizzie accepted the warm compassion that Zach so

generously gave but remained slightly aloof. She did not want to begin to create a strong dependence on some stranger who she knew nothing about, and who certainly knew nothing about her.

"Nevertheless, she accepted an invitation to go to the monthly dinner social at St. Michael's that Saturday and smiled warmly when she recognized his large frame standing behind the refreshment counter. The older Hungarian women huddled together, whispering approval that Zachariah had found some way to reach this young woman. She certainly was not like any that had come to the church hall before. She was not willing to accept the status quo and had ambition to try to become a success here in America.

"An immigrant and a woman, two strikes against her. What nerve! Well, perhaps Zach will quiet all those emotions down! A woman's place is in the kitchen," they harked.

Their courtship consisted of walks through Fairmount Park beside the Schuylkill River. Strolling hand in hand, they looked quite comical together: Zach's large six foot frame and Lizzie's plump five feet. He had helped to arrange some of the winter jasmine and kerrias which remained green in patches next to the garden path. He stooped to tenderly revive a red annual dianthus flower at the foot of a bare great oak. He was proud to have taken part in preparing the park to be the site for the Centennial Exposition in 1876. Lizzie was thrilled to be in this historic city where she had read that the actual signing of the Declaration of Independence took place.

"We can move into my home after we're married, Liz, and when I become owner of the florist shop, we can both run it."

A stream of protests poured forth from her nucleus.

"No, no, this is not in my plans at all. I have told you,

our marriage will not change my objectives. And if you do not agree, Mister, you can choose from any one of these women who will gladly do as you say, not me."

And that was final. Zachariah never again questioned the woman he loved. She was on a never-ending course and who was he to get in her way? Lizzie immediately felt saddened by her remark. She began to think she'd spoken too hastily.

"Perhaps we can have a restaurant with a garden throughout. That way we can both realize our ambitions. But for the meantime, let's go back to work and save to make them a reality."

They walked down to Spring Street, and then on toward the Hotel.

That evening, Zach potted vegetable seeds for spring planting. The black soil felt soft between his fingers, not much different from the coal dust that crawled in his eyes and ears as he targeted his coal mining pick into the black golden clusters jutting out before him. At fourteen he had been a strapping youth, physically vigorous and eager to help support his family. The mining cooperative had employed him and many other young men, even children to crawl into the tiny spaces necessary to find good coal veins for export. It was almost too late when he came to America to continue his skill in Wilkes-Barre since black lung and, later, emphysema was diagnosed. He applied for the florist position in Philadelphia in his weakened condition and happily regained almost total ease in breathing except for a nightly wheeze. Tantamount with his mining occupation, Zach had altered his disposition. He began to appreciate the dawning light of each new day, usually with seven o'clock mass. Equally, the spontaneity of life excited him in so many new ways. It had the power to pull him involuntarily in to everyday situations, like the run-away horse the day before yesterday. He had been busily watering the perennials when the neighing became distressingly prolonged. He ran onto the dirt road surrounding the greenhouse to sort the trouble out. The horse was being abused by its owner. Walking over to the horse and gently soothing and petting him, Zach brought peace and serenity to both the horse and owner who had become unjustifiably upset and had begun to swing the rampant whip relentlessly. These kinds of predicaments set Zach ablaze to get to the root of the trouble, especially when an unfortunate person or animal was at the receiving end. As big as he was, he was equally as gentle in nature. He would hold a delicate orchid in his hand, sensing its movement with his slight touch, wondering about the beauty of nature.

He wondered about the strange alliance between him and Lizzie. She was forceful, overbearing, domineering, headstrong, impulsive, and opposite him on every topic, things that would make any man run as fast as he could in the other direction. What was it about this woman that made him love her? She could certainly do without him. She was hell-bent on going forward with or without him. But he had his dreams, too, dammit. In many ways he wished he had never met Miss Elizabeth Kuchen. He hoped in the months ahead she would see that his way was best. She could cook for him and raise their children "American Style," whatever that was. Could Lizzie be this sensible? Well, he thought, he could bring her around with his easy going manner.

Christmas was different that year. "Dear Mama and Papa," Lizzie started her weekly letter telling news from her new country.

"America can be beautiful, with the excitement of Philadelphia with all the people going somewhere important every day, or the city can be cold as stone to foreigners like me, who are resented for even having stepped foot in to this country. It will take much time to establish myself here, but I am working in a good hotel with a future Assistant Chef position available." She wrote optimistically, but the truth was that Charlie, the head chef, did not want her as his assistant. He wanted a recent graduate of the French Cooking School, The Sorbonne, and planned to develop a variety of French Cuisine at the hotel, not Eastern European. She was beginning to get a little dismayed by his attitude toward her and wondered if she could alter her culinary skills in any way to include the art of French cooking. This was impossible, since he wanted that little certificate stating a person actually had graduated. It was clear to Lizzie that she should move on in the months to come. Belittling herself and her profession by cleaning pots was getting her nowhere, although Clara had begun to cultivate her more in the kitchen in the ways of food preparation. She knew that Clara was now on her side because she overheard her talking to Charlie one day, in her high pitched Irish brogue.

"Yer' gon't git that new assistant, an' thr goes y'r job, why don't ye' jst' put Lizzie in th'r, she's good as most, and she'll make ye' proud, mun."

But Charlie seemed stubborn about finding his new prize French Assistant. Lizzie felt that he was probably acting on hotel management orders. With ocean liners coming from every country daily, they probably wanted to bring their dining room standards up to other new romantic tastes. This rationale did not ease her feelings.

"I'm going to have to leave sooner than I thought. There must be a city nearby looking for some good cooks. And I have to try to make a little more money to save."

Zach met her discouragement with objectivity.

"Wilkes-Barre is a very busy mining city and plentiful European cooking like yours will be met with much appreciation."

Chapter 4 Moonshine

"What she don't know won't hurt 'er. We're gonna unload this jalopy and scram 'cause I'm gettin' the heebie jeebies," muttered Phil, "An' I don't want t' get pinched this time. Ma ain't gonna believe any more lines like th' I was framed story anymore. The lousy Feds are gonna be on our tail sniffin' out the hooch."

The moon shone overhead, spotlighting their quick underhanded movement of crates unloading the last of the liquid gold. It was the last stop on their run before Phil and Lonnie took off for a meeting with the boys. Just another speakeasy but it would net the owner a lot of money. The Feds would probably raid it. They all knew it took money to make money. The cost might go to $1,370 monthly—$400 for graft alone, to Federal prohibition agents, police department and District Attorney's. The cop on the beat also got another $40 to turn his back when the beer was delivered. They had found out at their last meeting with the "big boys" that a handful of Feds covered 18,700 miles of coastline and inland borders. Phil and the boys regarded the Feds with contempt since most of them would try to clean up the joints, making their job to keep them supplied harder. The Feds usually did their job honestly and conscientiously. All the local mobsters knew their habits, the Feds seized half a million gallons of hard liquor and almost five million gallons of beer nationwide in 1921; in 1925 they raised their haul to more than a million gallons of liquor and seven million gallons of beer. And most of the time a speakeasy was raided and padlocked in vain or "protected" for a monetary consideration.

Some members of Al Capone's gang were responsible for arranging the payoff. His organization was turned into a huge business at the top of a great terror-ridden pyramid, with operations by the end of the 1920's giving him a fortune of $40 million and his organization an income of $100 million a year. The booze would be bought up fast as women and men took up clandestine drinking. This appealing game became sport as they used ingenuity to get around the prohibition laws without getting arrested. Some used a hip flask, some hid it in false books, hot water bottles strung from their necks, garden hose wrapped around their waists, in babies prams or carpenter's aprons with big fat pockets, hollow canes, floppy overcoats and even in the new style thigh-high covered Russian boots.

Phil loved the thrill of making these deliveries to the "speaks" and they spoke to him of cold hard cash, but he didn't like draggin' that dame Maizie along, she asked too many questions, her squeaky voice always ending on that ugly high note. Then she takes a swig out of that silver flask of hers, swishin' the booze around in her mouth, not even asking them if they wanted any of the stuff.

Phil thought about his partner and friend, Lonnie; he was a handsome guy wearin' bow ties and sweaters, a smooth operator. He attracted those kind of flappers with their bobbed hair, short skirts and rolled down stockings flashin' their shapely gams. Yeah, Lonnie was a ladies's man and a push-over, with his black patent leather hair parted in the middle, he looked like some kind of movie hero. Those baggy knickers will look real snappy in his jail cell, if they get caught on this gig. Lonnie was real smart though, he should have gone away to school like his Ma wanted him to after eighth grade. But no, he just wanted to hang around with him. Now he'd have to be responsible for his soul, too. Well, he'd tried to warn him, and now Lonnie was in just as deep as he was in this bootleggin' racketeer business. They were both twenty and lusted for the dark side of life, knowing it could lead to life in prison.

But he wasn't as scared of Ma as he was of his saintly brother. Johnny had warned him the last time he was home from college, that he'd better not catch Phillie makin' those deliveries again. Yeah, Johnny was such a flat tire, what'd he know about the excitement he craved. Everything looked jake, as he twitched his dark wiry eye brows antennaeing out for any nearby Feds and quietly pulled the wheels of the jalopy on to the road. Lonnie and Maizie necked in the back which did throw off suspicion. Maybe it wasn't such a bad idea to bring the sheba along to be with her sheik, ha. They'd drop her off first at her swanky apartment on the main drag. She had some swell modern furniture and a bathroom with toilet paper to match, real hotsy totsy. Sometimes when they'd visit her, she'd wear them silk printed beach pajamas that showed off her shape, she bragged about not wearin' anything underneath. They stared at her chassis the whole time trying to glimpse a shot of something, but never could. Anyway, at least it was a way of avoiding looking at her face which looked downright spooky powdered up to a pallor mortis with scarlet lips and ringed eyes. She flaunted respectability, which didn't fit into the picture. That's why they thought she was keen. She kept them wondering about who actually kept her living in this grand style. They thought her Dad ran a gambling joint but she never talked about him.

"Are you fellahs gonna come up? We can roll back the rug and dance?"

"Lon can stay, I have to scram, the boys'll be havin' their bull session about now, kiddo."

Phil envied them a little for having their crush on each other. He was between bimbos right now. He wanted to get his professional life on the road. He'd had enough of the drugstore cowboy life trying to attract the gold-diggers. The women all thought he was a rich heir to a hotel fortune. Money flowed like rain in the hotel business, but it was hard work and that wasn't for him. He wanted easy money and it was out there for the askin'. Society was freewheeling and the mood seemed to be whatever a person wanted to get into. With Cal Coolidge running the government there didn't seem to be many business regulations, in fact, it seemed that Cal kept the status quo in order so that most people solved their own problems.

Relentless progress of the times left Phil and society, in general feeling disillusionment over government and religion; many put their sole interest in plans to make fast money. Materialism was his evangelism, the omnipotence of the almighty dollar, with faith in the supreme importance of automobiles and washing machines.

Phil pulled his hat down, mimicking Capone in a recent newsreel at the Rivoli Theatre. What a man, he thought. Capone called himself a businessman, not a racketeer.

"When I sell liquor, it's bootleggin', but when my patrons serve it on a silver tray on Lake Shore Drive, it's hospitality."

Al Capone had operations in every big city. Wearing his flashy pin-striped suits he spent big fat bankrolls on his friends and even the poor, his fortune was told to be in millions. He made the system work for him. Chicago respected him and so did Phil. No, the Feds'll never catch the big guy, Phil mused, he was too smart and too fast.

God was in his Heaven and all was copacetic with the world, as Dell crossed East Avenue passing the Albred Hotel on her way to work. Noticing Phil's jalopy parked in front with the motor still steaming, she wondered if all the stories she had heard about him were true. It seemed hard to believe that Johnny's younger brother could be mixed up in bootlegging whiskey. She knew him only to say hello to. She didn't know if he was a real McCoy bootlegger or not and didn't really care. There were too many wonderful things happening in her own life.

"Dell, the telephone is for you," Mabel sang across the desk.

Dell's face turned radish red as she reached for the receiver with all the office workers watching her with a crooked smile on their faces. Johnny had started calling her almost every day from college. She didn't know what had suddenly changed in his life, but somehow he had begun to realize he cared for her. She was elated at the attention he was paying to her. There was usually a beautiful letter waiting for her when she returned home from work which always began, "My Dearest Dell" oh, how that Johnny could write, right into her heart, words filled with the mastery of romance. The thought of him actually loving her warmed her down to the tip of her toes, transmitting sensations of energetic delight that would fill the tallest building of the world with brilliant warm sunshine. She had never felt this way before in her life. It was equal to the silent spiritual emotions she had in church on Sundays, especially after Holy Communion. It could only be described as a healthy glow of exhilaration, brought on by loving someone in a special way. Feelings that, indeed, made her love herself more. This new condition which was happening to her was unexplainable, but she felt so wonderful she wanted it to continue for the rest of her life.

They had corresponded long distance since he had left for school in September. Now, he would come home for the holidays and they would get to talk and sort out their future.

It had taken him at least three months to realize what she had realized in an instant that day in the garage. She hoped with all of her heart that she wasn't imagining it all, that she wasn't, as Ma would say, "in love with love". She worried some time that she wasn't sophisticated enough for this well-educated, interesting man. When he really got to know her, he would probably walk fast the other way. Never knowing what to say at the right time had always bothered her, whereas Johnny came equipped with all the perfect expressions to sail through every conversation. He made it all look so easy.

Even the gloomiest December days looked bright to Dell as she woke up for work on cold crisp mornings with the wren outside her window chirping an early morning song. Life had taken on new meaning for her since Johnny had begun to show serious interest in her. Before she met him, she didn't really like herself. She barely fit in with all the new wave of changing fashion. She knew lots of girls emulating the new flapper styles, but she wasn't one of them. Mary Pickford was her favorite movie star, with her long curls and pure and innocent look. She was somewhat kittenish, but she could also be bold and had confidence to face the man she loved with no assumption of consequences. Women were asserting themselves now—it was no longer strictly a man's world. They had finally won the right to vote and Dell had exercised hers in the last election.

Reading the new authors was her favorite pastime and great social writers of the day indoctrinated her to the world she never knew outside of her home. F. Scott Fitzgerald stretched her romantic imagination in *This Side of Paradise* which created a capacity for an escape into wonder. Conveying the fact that western society was being compelled into an aesthetic contemplation neither understood or desired, confused the modern day reader into wondering about where the material excesses of the day would lead. Edith Wharton's

Age of Innocence mocked high society in the 1920's. These different social stratas enabled Dell to compare her life with immigrant parents against another element of social development in America. These novels brought her in touch with the disenchantment all around her. In the Pulitzer Prize winning, *Age of Innocence*, the character of Countess Ellen Olenska laughs at the propriety imposed in the social standing of the upper classes and her portrayal of nostalgia in innocence lost forever in a new American way of life. Consequently, Dell was aware of negativity outside her own closed European social realm with friends and relatives breaking slowly into "normal" American lifestyles. When, in fact, American ideals presented in the 1920's were a lot of hokum and even great writers wrote this in an expatriotic vein. In 1921, Willa Cather recorded her thoughts on the standardization of American art forms. Cities looked alike with false conventions of thought and expression, machine-made art, superficial culture art from encyclopedias rather than experience "Human Sterility" devoid of creative color.

Creativity was held under wraps. Some of the outrageous which should have poured out into society was strained. T. S. Eliot's *Wasteland* provided evidence that directed toward turning a personal disappointment into a universal statement of civilized man's discontentment. The expatriot writers wrote from Europe, which increased the foreign demand for fountain pens, silk stockings, grapefruit and portable typewriters. Drawing after them an invading army of tourists, swelled the profits of steamship lines and travel agencies. The business picture all around was good. However, writers like Ring Lardner broke through the creative malaise with contemporary comic forms of writing. He breached the tie of elite class with common man. His prose stretched from American slang to Shakespearean English. His buoyancy was high and his underwater lines so fine as to lighten the conformity found in sterile working places like the Company where Dell worked. The image presented was one of looming opportunities for making a daily living with work and life laid out for a person, a form of stability. Cultivating men like Andrew Mellon, the Pittsburgh millionaire philanthropist who lived in grave elegance without display.

Dell's yearly salary as a stenographer of $2,000, stacked up with that of Federal employees making $1,375 in 1920 to $1,515 in 1924.

Maybe Mom had been right. She might have been "in love with love" at the outset, but she knew this feeling was right. The fact that a permanent relationship with John fit into this picture was based on him passing through her own ideals safely. Sometimes she did have uncertainties and, since they really hadn't actually sat down and planned a future together, maybe he even had other ideas about their relationship. She had gone on to think he wanted the same out of a relationship as she did. He might just want a good woman friend.

Dell was a trusting young woman and accepted most of the harsh realities of life. Because of her faith in God and humanity, her inherent goodness extended from a belief in her family to the fairness and honesty of the storekeepers and her fellow employees pouring out their troubles on to her generous, compassionate nature. She was a naturally optimistic loving person and could spread sunshine over the gloomiest of days, having only to be approached by a kind voice to respond with her gentle manner.

To say that she would be taken advantage of by people with this type of disposition was only half correct since this was an era where a good conscience still guided local society and where most people looked out for each other in their close ethnic area of Eastburgh. Consequently, she had many friends, and most looked forward to her presence in whatever way she touched them. Relationships with men ran from a strong father in Pop to Mr. Weatherby, her boss. Johnny was her first real contact with a man, beside the planned dates Aunt Pauline had made for her with a few "nice Slavic boys." And, even though Johnny lived in their same ethnic neighborhood, he had gone away to school when he was fourteen, which removed him from his former background.

Dell was well aware that procreation took place as a result of physical relations between men and woman. She just was not sure how this came about. She wasn't even sure about her own role in all this. She knew that men produced the seed to fertilize the egg and believed that physical relations between a man and a woman should be kept strictly inside the sacrament of marriage for the purpose of procreation. Sex for pleasure and fulfillment was out of her realm; consequently, she had no knowledge of sexual fulfillment whatsoever. The fact that Johnny would have any desires in this respect did not even enter her mind.

The Catholic Church had been her ultimate authority on the subject. Birth control was totally banned and Father Mayarek preached adamantly against it at every Sunday Mass. She did not know of any books written on the subject, but in 1921 people were beginning to question some of these traditional authorities that had reigned and controlled society.

Affluent social conditions of the decade seemed to be spawning a new breed who seemed to be hard boiled and heavy drinking, and most of her friends were changing with them. Cloche hats, silk stockings, open galoshes, short skirts, powdered knees, fake jewelry and bobbed hair replaced the flowing tresses of years ago. Couples now parked on dark roads to neck in struggle buggies, a car in which boys tried to seduce "nice" girls. Songs like "Runnin' Wild, lost control runnin' wild, mighty bold feeling, gay, reckless too," and "I'm the sheik of Araby, your love belongs to me at night when you're asleep, into your tent I'll creep."

Dell was confused. She had to follow her heart, but wasn't sure in what direction. She had heard about some girls in her neighborhood who had become flappers and were now pushing baby carriages down Cable Avenue. Their boyfriends were sent away to school or work—in most cases they didn't have to live with their "mistake" in the same way as the girls involved. Conclusively, Dell looked around herself at many things happening so fast and made up her mind that her life would be different. She would remain a virgin no matter what. Love did not necessarily have to be consecrated by sexual intercourse.

Through the grapevine, meaning Mrs. Rubash told Mrs. Gregoravich, who had spoken with Dell's mother in Krek's Butcher Shop, that Mrs. Lizzie Albred, the owner of the hotel's, son, Johnny was to become a priest, and that's why he had gone away to school at an early age.

Dell began to worry about these rumors. Johnny had led her to believe she was becoming important in his life. He never mentioned the priesthood once in any letter. The story went that Mrs. Albred, who had quite a reputation for being benevolent in religious circles, had actually wanted to sacrifice her first born to God, like the Biblical story of Abraham and Isaac at the Altar of God in the Old Testament. She was sure that this rumor had been circulated and dramatized in the words of old Mrs. Rubash, who had a marvelous gift of passing on information relating notorious events beginning with, "It is none of my business, but..." Dell found the complete allegory to be false from beginning to end, but she did intend to trace it together with Johnny. Perhaps its absurdity would open communication with him. God forbid that she should get in the way of him going into the religious life—she would rather die first! She also pondered the prospect of confronting Mrs. Albred, who did have ambitions for her son. Dell wondered how she would fit into this picture. Well, Johnny would handle it all properly in his gracious manner, she thought, as the beginning of an anxiety attack began to rumble in her weak stomach. "What if she had interrupted a vocation?" And with this, she made her way speedily to the bathroom.

In the meantime, in one of St. Vincent's oldest Fraternity Houses, George Gershwin's "Rhapsody in Blue," directed by Paul Whitman, blasted from an open window. Adulterating jazz through transmission of hungering and thrilling cadences meant only for youthful absorption pounded the walls. These uncivilized reverberations, pronounced by the older generation, emanated from KDKA radio in Pittsburgh. W. C. Handy's "St. Louis Blues," could bring lonely tears to most of their eyes, while Jack Teagarden improvised unidentified jam session originals complicated with a singing style all his own. Louie Armstrong, a young trumpet player from Chicago, had made some great phonograph records that the guys in the frat house had passed around, along with the swingin' cornet of Bix Beiderbecke, one of the few great white jazzmen of the time who had learned enough from the Negro musicians to cultivate a style of his own. What they liked the best about jazz was that it was not a learned musical style, but improvisational with notes being played in a harmonious pattern, or chords played by piano, guitar and string bass. Some roommates had jazz record collections which usually included one or two cornets, a trombone, clarinet, banjo or guitar, drum and string bass, led by Buddy Bolden, Bunk Johnson or Freddie Keppard.

However, at the top of the heap of all these greats, and Johnny's very favorite of all time, was not a jazz artist. John

Philip Sousa, America's most famous composer of band music, directing "The Stars and Stripes Forever" resounding from the school campus all the way into the city of Latrobe, Pennsylvania, had the worried Benedictines running toward vibrations originating from their frathouse. Sousa had led the United States Marine Corps Band from 1880 to 1892. During the Spanish-American War, Sousa served as musical director for the United States Army. Johnny had never been in any of the wars. He was not old enough for WWI and he really didn't have a military streak, but he thrilled with these marches and felt motivated toward good study practices through their cadence.

"John Aloyisius Albred, you are bordering on expulsion from the college and all ground activities herein!" came the brassy voice of Father Raymond Barone, prefect assigned to them for that year.

"Father, I have been studying so hard here that I haven't taken notice of the loud volume," Johnny responded as he shone his large brown eyes toward the monk's beleaguered stance.

"John, I am impressed with the concentrated realm which your study has taken you, but the town is complaining about the tumultuous sound waves vibrating against their houses. Now, Johnny I do not want to make a repeat visit to your room."

Once again Johnny had been saved from the wrath of the Benedictine fury.

He knew he could charm even the most obstinate and often tried to test his ability in the most unique of ways like getting out of the most difficult situations with his smooth persuasive semantics. It was his sales ability, blending a colorful story with the facts and a little peppering of humor gave the added touch to his trusting audience. The sober, uncompromising features of his face, elicited any response to the perfectly legitimate conveyance of rhetoric. His friends laughed at his cunning way with words and predicaments. They brought their complex school problems to him like getting out of an exam in Ethics they had not studied for or what to tell their parents about their low mid-semester grades.

Across the country, salesmanship had become the greatest of the performing arts. And Johnny had the resources which Sinclair Lewis facetiously called "the cosmic purpose of selling." A bestseller called *The Man Nobody Knows* by Bruce Barton put forth the startling thesis that the title character, Jesus, was the world's greatest salesman. He had power to pick men with hidden capacities in them, the disciples: A haphazard collection of fishermen, small-town businessmen, and one distinctly hated element in the community, the tax collector. Their product wasn't even tangible since it was the philosophy of Christianity. The book presented, however, a confusing philosophy for the liberated theologian which Johnny prescribed himself to be. In conjunction with this, he spent a lot of his time attacking some of the evils of materialism.

The meaning of theology itself was a Greek word which means the study of God and achievement of a deeper understanding of the revelation that is in the Bible. He felt that consumerism and secularism eroded the pureness of the spirit within a person and Johnny, as all young men his age, began to appreciate the "finer things coming about in the decade of the twenties, especially the auto," as underneath a deep disdain for the erosion caused in the spiritual side of society would grow more apparent to him as he matured. His consistent conscience would battle within him regarding good and evil. In the years ahead he would dichotomize between both, mostly seeing material pleasures as evil, bringing most of the ethics of Christian philosophy and teachings of the Benedictine Monks into everyday life.

His new feelings of love for a woman had entered Johnny's everyday world. Between or before studies he wrote or called her. She consumed most of his thoughts for the future, however, he was bothered by the fact that another woman lurked in the shadows of his mind: His mother. A dissertation on "Pursuing the life you were meant to live," kept writing itself out in his mind, reeling into the context of a form that would reach his Mother's mind. She would certainly be difficult to reach from an academic standpoint on individualism which was the level from which he wished to communicate. He was proud of her accomplishment, she had risen from the lowest peasantry class in Europe. But, he was sure she would understand the idea but not the application. For when it came to him, she had a one track mind. She would never see him as an average Joe with a love story to tell. Even when he had told her how he had met a women, fallen in love, maybe even marriage was in the offing, she would demand continuous explanation. She might even condemn the marriage and him with that venom only she could spew. But, most likely she would accuse him of carrying a torch and say, "you'll get over it, it happens to all of us one time or another." She would be disappointed with failing plans that he was supposed to carry out. But, why was it his responsibility? Time would tell. Next week was the beginning of Christmas Holiday and at least he would see his lady love. He was prepared to love her openly—no more hiding. He would make that clear to the world.

Escapism for Johnny came in the form of a game with Navy that rainy afternoon, his mind and heart punted into another spectacular form of excitement and one of the loves of his life, football. The non-stop action pulled him in emotionally through the plays of their home team, the St. Vincent Bears. They were four and 0 and showed great promise of bringing in the title. The other team might win today but they'd have a hell of a battle on their hands. It was a compulsory rule of the school that student cheering take place. They had to get behind the team which forced all the disgruntled students to the game.

One of the current coaches he admired was Knute Rockne of Notre Dame. They had won almost all of their games and his high—jinx in the locker room always made interesting reading in the sports pages, as Grantland Rice wrote about "outlined against a blue-gray October sky, the Four Horsemen rode again." These sports figures were the stuff that legends came from.

Ma had seen to it that he didn't play but that didn't mean that he couldn't watch and fight on in spirit for the rowdy home team. Most of the new first string were guys on athletic scholarship sought out from the new ethnic minorities, brought in from other parts of the country. They were an interesting crew and brought a new name to the game. Normally they might have gone from vocational high school to shoveling slag in a steel mill, but other alumni offered to pay their board and supply pocket money while physical education departments took care of their tuition. Some sportswriters had even written that the roster of Notre Dame's Fighting Irish looked like the telephone directory of Warsaw. This opportunity to play and learn in the big leagues paved the way for minorities and future economic gains.

Johnny knew a few of these guys around campus and usually had to chuckle when their families visited them with a basket loaded with kielbasa. Pungent spices and garlic permeated the halls. He wondered how this college life would divide the European American world they lived in. Since some of the advantages here were not connected with learning, the new celebrated way of life brought with it a lot of hero-worship and lots of victory delight over worthy opponents. There was also special attention from girls and the privilege of getting away with more bunk on campus, which unnerved Johnny and Jack. Just because they were winning games, the school didn't give them the right to become gate-crashers.

The new ethnic variety were socially unrefined in many ways, and their lousy manners became lousier as the night wore on. It wasn't as though they were lost causes, they just weren't cultivated into any kind of social refinement.

At the end of the fourth quarter the team really started to move, as Bill Dombroski ran forty yards for a touchdown to break the tie and win the game. Screams of jubilation filled the stadium as the players scrambled all over each other. That night the Victory Dance was one big boisterous affair, when some of the sheba's got loose and climbed on top of a table to dance, the sheiks began to cluster around her and shouted, "Get hot!" Meanwhile, some of the new heroes rushed in and tried to maul the little hoofers. Jack, Al, and Johnny had to try to keep order.

"Control yerselves, yore not on the field now, it's time to just watch for a while."

They didn't know whether they got the message or not, but it took three or four of them to throw them out sometimes, especially when the big gorillas had some hooch in them. The women from the nearby St. Joseph's College dressed according to administration regulations with suitable underslips for thin dresses, and skirts that didn't expose the calf of their leg. No thin or flesh-colored hose was permitted. Watching the new dances played by the college jazz band, "In the mornin' in the evenin' ain't we got fun" and "Five Foot Two, Eyes of Blue," the men staring steadily at their slim silhouettes moving to the black bottom, shimmy, and the Charleston which usually forced them to "park their girdles" somewhere first as their torsos required vigorous agitation.

The rhythmically maneuvering dancers moved closer to them and Johnny's thoughts returned to the thin, long lines of the plain and ordinary woman he loved. Her freshly-washed, unpowdered face gleamed in the sun with a meagerness and, yet, a rugged tomboyishness that made him conscious of the possible consequences of more exciting intimacy. Even though their two bodies had not touched yet, he had begun to feel her beside him.

At the beginning of this semester, they had a lecturer at the school on the findings of John Watson, America's leader at the time on behaviorist psychology. He regarded love as an art and not an instinct, which was disputed by many but did progress the science past some of the previous misrepresentations of Freud. He brought some sexual repressions into the limelight. Even at the age of ten, children were encouraged to explore the sexual nature of their bodies. Johnny did not agree with the blatancy proscribed, but he did feel that an open honesty about one's body was somewhat normal. A pregnant woman was God's plan for procreation and if his son was curious about sex education it was his right to know. This would definitely breed a healthier environment in the home. But it would have to be followed up with two loving, supportive parents. Sexual behavior had come a long way from the dark ages, but only in the secular world and not the priesthood. Johnny had finally surmounted the last hurdle of his decision to marry. The Vatican had rarely broached the world of human sexuality and yet it was looming stronger than ever in a more promiscuous world. The dogma and conservatism of the church offended him with its institutional rigidity when the very human souls that they dealt with had a sexual core and they were advised to ignore that center.

A wave of clean air circled around him when he folded a sweater and put it on the last pile of clothing to be put into his suitcase for transport home, together with clear resolutions made for the future. After all, he was his own man. He had love, and they had a wonderful future together.

Chapter 5 Confrontation

"Ma, I checked the rooms on the second floor, and they look good. Rosey did a good job up there."

Lizzie knew Aggie's idea of a "good job" would not pass her own inspection. She couldn't trust her own daughter to have her same high standards in the rigors of keeping an impeccable establishment, not just for a good reputation in the city, but so that they would be ready at all times for the health inspector's unannounced visit. Clean bedsheets for forty-seven rooms were unfolded and tucked under mattresses daily before the dusting and scrubbing took place. A rubbed-to-a-shine brass spindle bed, small mahogany night table with writing paper and a small lamp were the only fixtures present in the spotless little rooms. Every inch, especially corners, in the narrow dark closets were checked regularly for a natural enemy: bedbugs, which resulted in strong maneuvers with cyanide mixture. Windows were thrown open to release the noxious agents to prevent asphyxiation of the soon-to-be-arriving guests, together with the twenty-five permanent residents. The eye-watering fumes permeated bed clothes, walls, wood and pores of everything, even after wiping clean with Lizzie's homemade glycerin soap. Summer brought fresh air between arrivals of the train from the Pennsylvania Railroad behind the hotel and pollutants exhaled from the giant Westinghouse Electric Plant situated directly across the street.

Winter would not allow for the usual air flow which, when mixed with food cooking, disavowed liquor, tobacco smoke, spittoons, and the potent consummate mixture of humans. On a rainy, closed-window day, the formidable blast upon opening the front door could impale a newcomer in to doing a swift turn about return to the sidewalk.

Aggie assisted the paid help. There were two other Slovak girls who spoke no English. Aggie had stopped going to school in the sixth grade—her own choice—convincing Lizzie that she would spend time working and supervising the rest of the help at the hotel. Lizzie, taken in one of her rare weak moments, had believed her daughter. Now she thought back with regret at her lenience swaying toward her Aggie's whim, five years ago. Why had she been so strict with Johnny, and yet, had let Phil and Aggie have so much freedom? Aggie would most likely marry and Phil would keep the hotel going long after they were gone. But Johnny would fulfill her promise to God made back in the church in her village of Moila.

"Ma, I'm going down to Sach's," Aggie shouted from the open door. Sach's on Fourth Avenue was the most exclusive women's store in town. What would become of that girl, Lizzie thought: All she was really good at was spending money. She exhibited no business sense whatsoever and Lizzie was not sure what her inherent talent was. Lizzie would have to steer her toward finding a good husband to support her expensive tastes. A beautiful girl with long wavy auburn hair falling to her shoulders, Aggie removed the dust cap she detested. High rounded cheek bones defined natural rosy cheeks emphasizing a milk-white flawless complexion which never knew artificial coloring of any kind. Naturally, she wore the latest fashion of the day which enhanced her well-endowed figure as most of the male residents noticed with approval. Their piercing eyes would undress her with leers from the bar. These did not bother Aggie, who kept them in line with just a sharp look, well before Lizzie had a chance to react on behalf of her daughter's dignity. A beautiful young woman with a body bordering on the chubby side, she would smile and laugh with the customers but never sit with them. She was not promiscuous and was discriminating about who she went out with. Lizzie had just begun to permit her to go for a ride or walk with a young man alone, but he had to come and meet them first. And usually, she would investigate his family background.

The times were going too fast for Lizzie in the hedonistic culture they were living in compared with the slow and meager lifestyle where she had grown up in Eastern Europe. Lizzie knew she had paid all of her attention to the business and none to her family. Ever since she and Zach had moved in 1885 from Philadelphia to Wilkes-Barre and then to Eastburgh, she sometimes worked twenty hours a day to make a good living.

"Zach, I will never be able to start a good business out in those woods." She remembered hearing stories of Indians still raiding villages on the outskirts of town.

"Lizzie, I have never seen an Indian in all the years I worked in the mines there. Most of them are further west from here."

They peeked out of the train window leaving Philadelphia and then Harrisburg, toward great dim buildings and houses with shuttered eyes. Billboards with gaudy ads close against the train windows then lonely street lamps on streets of scattered houses streaked past. A large expanse of telegraph poles told their lengths of wire announcing the enormous gray ashy slopes of coal mines where stars appeared like sparkling cinders. Settling back into his Pullman, Zach remembered Wilkes Barre and his former coal mining days. But now it would be different. He and Lizzie had finally agreed on a lucrative business they could run together. They would pull their instincts and learn what did not come naturally for the success of the small town green grocer. The former owner had said the customer potential was at least fifty thousand gross yearly, with the cost of the rent it was affordable. He also had a small savings for emergency only which he had not told Lizzie about.

They would also sell yard goods, hardware and canned goods from the farm products which would come in abundance during the harvest seasons. Lizzie could also sell her baked goods and perhaps they could open a small restaurant next door later as they grew more prosperous. There was a small settlement of German and Hungarian farmers who would bring their produce and some meat there to market and also display the finer goods such as homemade crocheted and knitted items. Lizzie would have a chance to develop better speaking English and rapport with Americans outside of the urban areas.

Since their quiet church wedding the month before, Lizzie had begun to observe the reserved manner Zach displayed in business matters.

"You cannot trust these men to deliver their goods on time, unless it is here in writing." She hit the note pad with her pencil point.

But Zach was true to his friends and fellow countrymen, saying, "They're good men, their word is as good as their signature."

This was why Lizzie went about business in her own way covering his tracks; he knew her suspicious nature and didn't seem to mind as she was more aware of human frailty than he allowed himself to be. Zach enjoyed being with the hard-working people of the neighborhood and when he wasn't doing the heavy work of lifting sacks of stores into the open barrels for customers or tending to the outside store and barn repairs, he liked socializing with customers best.

"Thank you, Mrs. Green, I knew you would like the new canned peaches just in from Atlanta. Yes, I'll let you know when the new printed percale arrives from Burlington Mills for your daughter's school dresses. How are Sophie and Mildred?"

Lizzie, too, was beginning to enjoy the camaraderie with the customers as she spoke with them in her best broken English. Working to please the customers was paramount as she arranged the small general store with desired goods in the front. Zach could usually be found sitting around the potbellied stove most mornings and evenings with husbands while their wives sorted out their much needed household goods with Lizzie.

"Do you have the new wide-mouth Mason Jars for canning tomato relish and piccalilli?"

"No, but we have ordered several cases and they will be here at end of the month," Lizzie insisted.

Zach listened with pride, saying to himself, "She is learning the American way of business, and even though she is not doing exactly what she wanted to do, cooking for her grand restaurant, look at the experience she is getting as customers come and go everyday."

Negotiating with salesmen also became a new way of life for Lizzie as she bargained for a better price.

"No, I will not pay a penny more for that peck of nails, our customers cannot afford it and neither can we."

Some of the second shift miners came for lunch as Lizzie cooked over the enormous coal-fed Franklin Stove. Stews and soups served together with hot biscuits and homemade breads satisfied their bellies and billfold tantamount.

Their general store, situated at the beginning of town, was just down the hill from the busy Number Four mine. The shrill sounds of the emergency mine whistle shook the town at any hour of the day, screaming out to the people, as mothers, wives, and sisters ran to the opening of the black tomb of hard coal. Lizzie and Zach were the first to run out to anxious family members with provisions of coffee, soup, blankets and supplies. Nearly all the male population of the town worked in the lucrative anthracite mines of Pennsylvania, from the early age of eleven or twelve years old. Most had years of coal dust embedded in their pores, under fingernails and throughout raspy voices and lungs. Mining from cradle to grave consumed all their lives, as generations followed the same pattern. These were the same mines that had attracted Zach to America five years before. Lizzie breathed a sigh of relief that he no longer had to ingest the black dust into his lungs; it was bad enough that they lived this close to one of the sources of the emphysema he had developed, especially since he had started in the mines at a very young age in Hungary.

Their first year in Wilkes Barre completed, Lizzie found herself expecting their first child. She hid her bulky weight behind a large full apron. Embarrassment and self-consciousness followed her everyday as concerned patrons strained to help her in her uncomfortable position of moving around the well-stocked store. As much as the natural process of childbearing was a part of everyday life, she wondered why it caused such suspense and curiosity. She had decided not to hide her swolleness, but instead to continue to work behind the counter and kitchen pretending everything was normal. Many women wore black during pregnancy and most stayed indoors laying in wait for the blessed event. One of the men commented on her boldness.

"Why doesn't your wife stay in the back more now? It's shocking how she parades out in the open with her big stomach. No decent woman would do such a thing."

"Lizzie is a businesswoman, we have work to do here, and God created women to bear children. Now do you want to buy anything here or not?" Zach had said his piece customer or no, but his frustrations got the best of him later as

Lizzie found him sullen, stacking cans on the top shelves.

"That damn Frances Benning, sticking his nose in where it doesn't belong again. What a pain in the ass? He never had any children, that's probably why he's jealous of us. Some of these people are not satisfied until they spread their anger all around."

This was one of the few times Lizzie had seen Zach angry. Frances Benning was never seen in the store again. Zachariah Albred had had about enough of the insults from men like him, not just toward his wife, but all the comments he had made in the past about women in general. They wanted to take their hatred out on women, whether it was because women had mistreated them in some way, or that they were unhappy about something in their own lives, he wasn't sure. But it just wasn't right. He and Lizzie shared the same respect for each other; they were helpmates.

On Christmas Day 1901, John Aloyisius Albred was born in an old wooden attic upstairs above the general store, a plump little boy cherub born to Elizabeth and Zachariah. The significance of this occasion brought Lizzie in touch with her covenant and pronounced him one of God's own immediately after his birth. He would be the beginning of their first generation in America, destined to go forth and preach God's word. And nothing else would be good enough, she would see to that. No coal mines for him; his would be spiritual work.

Little Johnny was everywhere; from crawling and playing behind the pickle barrels, to sitting in the middle of a carload of miner's shoes. He grew up in the middle of commerce. Walking and talking at an early age, he was a precocious preschooler running simple errands responsibly for Lizzie and Zach.

"I delivered Mr. Garnish's milk in my wagon, Mom.

Now I'll help Daddy clean out back."

He knew all the prices by heart, as some children know their nursery rhymes. Lizzie would ask him the cost of some of the smaller items.

"Johnny, how much are these tomatoes a pound"?

"Ten pennies," he would answer, or "Two bits," for another product.

And when Lizzie found that she was expecting her second child, she felt comfortable in the fact that Johnny was around to help. He was a robust, good-natured boy, eager to get involved with everything going on around him.

"Johnny's enthusiasm will carry him far in America. Mr. Ashmont, the Bookkeeper at the Miners Bank, replied one day, as he purchased a spool of red thread for a dress his wife was sewing. "His attitude seems to be what is necessary for success here. He has that positive outlook to achieve success in life."

But there were times when Johnny, at his young age, would grow impatient with his father, trying to encourage him to be more motivated in business.

"Come on, Dad, let's put the flour and other baking staples in the front for customers to see since Easter will be coming next month, The women in the town will see them there as soon as they enter the store."

Zach knew the boy had a good business sense, not just from the produce side, but also from meeting and greeting people as they came into the shop.

"Hello Mrs. Garish, what can we do for you today? Have you seen the new zippers that have just come in from Chicago? You can put them on your husbands pants or jacket when you make them for their church clothes."

Zach was sitting in the back at the roll-top desk nearly hidden from the rest of the store, searching the long ledger book for the unpaid monthly bills, but he couldn't help chuckling as he filled his pipe, at the boy's acumen. He certainly knows how to manipulate the purchasing power of people's minds, he thought. Immelda Garish, an affluent farmer's wife from the country, inspected the newly invented closure as Johnny demonstrated over and over again. His small hands grasped the cloth sides in an upward manner gently moving the lever on the closure for her observation.

"I'll buy two of those, for suit pants I'm making. What other new merchandise do you have new in today?"

Johnny ran to get a white plastic bowl brought in by a New York manufacturer.

"Oh, I don't know about this, it looks a little weak, won't it crack if I put something hot into it?"

He had pushed it too far this time, he didn't know enough about the new material "plastic" that had just been invented. Zach came to the front and added up her purchases. Sales had come to almost twenty dollars that morning.

"You did well, Johnny, you're a good salesman out here."

Johnny smiled up at his tall Papa. He had such a large handle bar mustache, that most of the time Johnny was not sure if his mouth underneath was smiling or not. But Zach was perplexed now, as he wondered from time to time why Lizzie wanted him to be shut away in some seminary someday. He was a sociable young boy with an intuition for people's buying motives. He should not be locked away with God somewhere in a dark church.

Johnny's new selling virtue took a different turn when his daily chores took on the responsibility of looking after his baby brother, Phil, who seemed to get into everything. One day Phil even managed to get into a barrel of oats, throwing the loose seeds all over the back of the storeroom and having a high old time with Johnny running to pull him away from the mess.

"What do you think you're doing, fellah?" He cried, as the baby boy's gleeful laugh traveled away from the scene.

He seemed to take delight at the outset of his life by causing distress for attention. Since Lizzie and Zach paid almost no attention to the new baby, Johnny usually was the one to discipline. They didn't seem to mind because they were both too busy buying and selling for the store. When his mother was not out front, she would be baking pies and cooking or balancing the accounts in the back room. It was to his consternation that Zach did not share as much of the work as he could have, but his father always comforted Lizzie when she was sad, even though he wasn't altogether well with the constant wheeze he carried everywhere.

Lizzie was almost content with her life until she found out about a restaurant/hotel for sale in western Pennsylvania near Pittsburgh.

"Zach, it's located across from the new Westinghouse Electric Plant in East Pittsburgh! Mr. Kovacik said it has a lot of business promise."

She had kept in touch with Kovacik over the years, who continued to look out for their little group. He had written about the new plant hiring many new immigrants everyday for their special apprentice skills acquired in eastern Europe. What's more, Mr. George Westinghouse himself was there to greet them. The comfort of being amongst those of their own nationality and the prospect of finally opening her hotel spurred Lizzie into action. She was becoming more deeply affected by being uprooted from her culture, especially since their food was not really accepted by main stream America. The ritual gatherings of people at mealtime together with the food was what made her cooking worthwhile. Food was the center of their culture—that was why she enjoyed cooking so much. The good times associated with mealtime in Europe made it a joy to sit down and eat good food and drink fine wine while discussing the progress of the day. It was a happy spiritual time, when grace was said and friends and family gathered. Here in America the cultural value was lost, not because they didn't appreciate what God had done for them, but because they ate because they had to, not for the sheer pleasure. People did not take time to savor the meal and good fellowship involved. It just wasn't the same. She delighted in the fact that she and Zach might be able to recapture some of those moments with the customers they would attract to the establishment.

The store wouldn't be difficult to sell and just the thrill of sitting down and planning menus for the clientele excited her. It would be an opportunity of a lifetime and a chance to get back into the mainstream of society again.

She promised Zach it would be their last move. Knowing he was happy in their present location, she thought he might sulk about going as he did when not entirely in agreement. This attitude bothered her more than an outright argument. The dream of his flower shop always came back hauntingly in her dreams. She would see him pulling a cart of flowers through her restaurant or trying to sell flowers to customers, but just as they reached for them they would turn into a popover or a kifli pastry. Zach never outwardly expressed any unhappiness with any of her plans but would thoughtfully smooth his full bristled, handle-bar mustache. Lizzie would look into his kind eyes and try to cajole him into the exciting prospect of taking charge of the hotel bar and associate with new customers and, since he was naturally personable he could sympathize with the difficult times the new arrivals encountered in America, and maybe even advise them.

"Mother, I have just heard a rumor in Sach's that our Johnny has been writing and calling the Gesner girl...boy, are my dogs tired," Aggie shouted, stuffing her rustling packages into a red velvet tufted Victorian lounge chair.

Peering into a mirror above the marble-topped table near the entrance of the dark mahoganied hallway, she retouched an auburn curl that fell over her eye as she removed her tight-fitting cloche.

"Yeah, they say our Johnny is carrying a torch from way up there in Latrobe. Those Rubash girls tried to give me more details about how starry eyed this Dell is at the Plant and all that, but I just snubbed them and told them they were all wet. I said my Mother wouldn't let Johnny fall in love with some dumb dora when he's gonna be a priest. I said go fly a kite, that's a lotta bunk."

As she turned to open her nearest package, a heavy force came down upon her arm pulling her weight in two motions back through the hall and into the small office at the end of the hall, far away from the nosy lunchtime patrons. Stumbling backward clumsily, almost loosing her balance, Aggie slowly regained momentum turning around to look directly into intense piercing brown eyes. Recalling the strength of her Mother who brought herself up much taller than her five foot frame, Aggie began to tremble from within. Her Mother's strong, developed arms crossed over her chest resembling two sharp butcher knives from her impeccable kitchen.

"Who started this vicious rumor?" Lizzie thundered. "What kind of gossip is this? Who has time for this kind of bad talk?"

Aggie had only seen her Mother this mad once before, and that was when she caught Zach with the upstairs maid. She wasn't really frightened of her Mother, just worried she would say the wrong thing and get herself deeper in trouble in the process.

"I don't know Mom I only know they were talking

about Johnny and Dell having some kind of a romance by mail, it doesn't mean its true, it's probably just a rumor. Besides, how much courting can you do by mail and phone? They're probably just friends." Aggie shakily tried to appease her mother's anger but knew it was useless.

Lizzie was her own containment and it was airtight. Being her own person, no one could penetrate her iron will. When she was angry or sad, she had to find her own solutions the same as she would have to find out the truth to this hokum being spread around about John. As Lizzie reached for the phone, Aggie slithered away quietly through the half-opened door. She knew it would be Johnny's head on the line. Lizzie told the operator the number, then stopped, realizing that Johnny would be home in a week for Christmas vacation. That was when she would face him. Maybe he was just having a little fling of some kind; it couldn't amount to much, but what about his studies? A smart boy like him going for this a little gold-digger. I'll get to the bottom of it sooner or later she thought. There'll be no marriage for him. Terrible, disheartening thoughts circled her mind bringing her to ill-conceived notions, like where had she gone wrong? She shouldn't have permitted him to work in that garage during the summer. He had come in contact with the wrong people, like this Gesner girl. She was sure this she-devil tempted him, enticing him into her net everyday. She would deal with this detestable young woman. And God would punish her for luring one of his intended priests away from the church.

Hoagie the hotel handyman, dragged in huge boughs of evergreen to the bar for Christmas trimming. Felix Washington Hoag had blown in on a strong wind from South Carolina one summer. No one was quite sure how he arrived on the scene, except that from Day One a southern drawl was showing up in a lot of the newly spoken English words tried in conversation by the more imaginative immigrants.

"Y'all git me a bier nah, Zach, y'hear," spoke Nathaniel Greenburg, a German-Jew now in permanent residence there.

Mixtures of accents were vocalized around the hotel, as if a choir from the league of nations had an informal meeting there every day. Politics, sports, religion, and women (when Lizzie wasn't around) were just some of the topics discussed by the distinguished men of the bar which included Czechs, Hungarians, Germans and Irish.

"America is not an easy country in which to get rich."

This was one subject the hard working men from the steel mills and plants agreed on. Whether or not one went to Purgatory after death drew a deep philosophical religious discussion. Sports were paramount too, if "The Babe" would beat his record of 59 home runs in 1921 brought excitement during the season, but most of the men cried about their remaining families in Europe. Pictures were shown and plans were openly made about how to finance trips to the United States and where to live after doing so. The hotel was open only to single residents, not whole families. Once in a while Lizzie bent her rules, but the families were accepted for limited periods of time before they found a permanent place to live.

Reigning supreme as head of these discussions-in-residence was his eminence, Zachariah. Standing behind the huge ring-stained wide mahogany bar, his authority reflected in the huge gilt-trimmed mirror. His high tied white starched apron reaching mid-chest gleamed as he ruled in favor of the jurors. Lizzie might have been queen of the kitchen, but Zach's empire took in the bar and visiting dignitaries. An important established rule he imposed was that tobacco smokers and chewers must hit the shiny brass spittoon and not the floor. "No Profanity," a sign to the left of the bar mirror said. Lizzie would enforce that one, since Zach would usually ignore any serious, rambunctious bar room confrontation, and Lizzie knew his control did not transcend his mahogany monarchy.

There were two other hotels in the "burgh," but none so ideally located across from the main plant. Supervisors and foremen came here for lunch or drinks after work. Zach would make special arrangements with them and personnel agents to have their new employees stay there where it would be somewhat like home.

Zach waited with excitement at the thought of his oldest son coming home for the holidays.

"Hi ya, Pop," Phil shouted as he pushed open the swinging doors, entering with some of his questionable chums. "How 'bout fillin' up some glasses for us?"

Pop turned around while wiping a glass clean.

"Sure, but they're not free this time. Get your cash ready."

The difference between Johnny and Phil were like day and night. Johnny was fair-faced with fine sandy-colored hair, while Phil had dark wavy hair and shifty eyes. Phil reminded Zach of the Gypsies he knew who frequented the slums of Budapest. He always had some scheme tucked up his devious sleeve. One of his biggest had brought business in during tough times at the hotel. Secretly, Zach wished Phil would take more of an interest in the business part of the hotel since he would probably be the one to inherit it someday, but Lizzie kept her iron hand on all finances. He wasn't twenty yet, but had done business with and even looked like a genuine copy of Capone himself, with his dark felt Stetson and flared camel coat. His connections with the bootlegging establishment kept them in quality liquor. But the real barrier between the bar and the law was Sal Peterson, the Prohibition Officer. A small, thin, mousy person, Sal slipped in and out before he could be spotted, downing his shot and a beer in a sharp split second. He came from a long line of crooked Eastburgh cops who knew how to keep the Feds away. He would usually arrive on the scene to exceptional hospitality, including free food and drinks, not unlike what Father O'Flaherty, the Pope and President rolled into one would receive. But, this ploy was in appearance only, since, soon after he left, everyone talked about what a louse he was with all the graft he was extorting from them.

Regardless, he served his purpose by tipping Zach off any time of day the Feds made their rounds. Usually a note with a big red "X" sufficed. With this, he would get word out early so that Zach could push a hidden button behind a gleaming crystal decanter, releasing a gear that rotated the huge bar around to the other side, hiding all the illegal booze long before the authorities appeared. Then he brought out the ginger ale, sarsaparilla, cappuccino and other would-be substitute exotic refreshments. One of the problems with Sal, though, was the special attention he paid to Aggie. He would openly call her "Mary," after film star Mary Pickford. Aggie, of course, realized this, thrilling at the attentions from this "hotel celebrity," sometimes assuming a posture of M.P. herself, with her long auburn hair hanging wavingly restless over one eye, her new short shirt creeping up to reveal chubby knees under her new metallic stockings. But in Zach's mind she looked more like his little girl being set up by their ticket to a booming business. Therefore, he did what any good businessman would do—Alert his wife, Lizzie, about the effect that Sal brought out in Agatha.

"Stay away from that man, he's got a wife and kids, besides he's a business associate of your father's," Lizzie would scold.

"Aw, Ma, we're just havin' a little fun, I don't believe his line," Aggie said, sorry their little playfulness was found out.

But she thought that Sal had sex appeal, even if he looked like a sneaky guy she wouldn't even begin to trust.

She was no pushover. She wanted a man with money and a big car. If he was tall and handsome it would be keen, but nothing else was required. She could fill in the rest with her sensational personality. She wanted a swanky kind of life like Gloria Swanson in her "Gilded Cage," or Pola Negri and especially Mary Pickford. She knew her long curls looked just like Mary's but maybe she would have them bobbed like Gloria Swanson.

"Hey kiddo, whad ya' go an' tell on Johnny like dat to Ma?" Phil spouted, as she handed him his drink from the bar.

At this remark she went to center stage again, placing both hands on her hips.

"Why should Johnny be havin' all the fun? He's the one with the hotsy-totsy life, the big cheese livin' away from all this mess. I hate this old speak-easy. Besides, I just told it like I heard it. He's got a royal crush on that Gesner girl, I just got Mom hep to it."

With that she walked away with her bottom lip out in full resentment of the favored treatment they all knew Johnny had always received from their Mother.

The bare hills scattered over the sooty city. Pittsburgh pitted itself against monumental blasts of industrial explosion at the turn of the century, harbinger of success to Lizzie, Zach, Johnny and Philip Albred arriving on the Baltimore and Ohio Railroad to its two dismal rivers uniting to form a third. Stone jutted out of the larger mountains, holding enormous cottages of 1880's architecture boasting Scotch-Irish independence. A small boy in a sweater could be seen sitting at schoolwork at an upper window, his legs hanging out toward a roof. Vacant houses with huge recesses, and gravestones from another era lined the dingy cliffs, portending tribute to passed-on giants of revolution. Golden flames spotlighted the Carnegie Steel Works, while the Heinz factory in Allegheny bubbled with enormous vats of tomato ketchup and pickles of every variety, fifty-seven, all told. CRUICKSHANK APPLE BUTTER presented itself on billboards, next to the pillaring inclines moving upward to the celestial heights of Mount Washington. The faces of the people had a coal-dusted sheen about them, blending into the gray, ashy day in January. The tough life they led was exhibited in their cold dark eyes. The men with their mechanical fierceness, steely slang and voices with the "Pittsburgh wise-cracks" could be heard echoing through the hollowed out hills. Front lawns depicted cinder piles, grass roots sealed permanently for another era, while women swept porches relentlessly. Trains and factories hooted at the hard hills remote in the west, cutting off culture and beauty. Little brick houses stood like jails at the bottom of the smoke-smothered gully. While factories spouted vapors of gold over dingy cliffs lined with flimsy dwellings like blackened barnacles left by the rush of tide. It was a city where country met country, a mixture of nationalities struggling to hold on to a dream of freedom in a new culture acting out the only rule they had rehearsed for the time being.

The steel industry had blazed the trail for central establishment of many new companies like the enormous Westinghouse plant. It started with the invention of the air brake for railroad trains, perfected in 1868. George Westinghouse also invented alternating current for electric power transmission and a system of pipes to conduct natural gas into homes safely. He also invented the gas meter. By 1866 he had already perfected two inventions: a device for replacing derailed railroad cars and railroad frog, an X-shaped device to enable the wheels running on one track to cross the rail of another track which made it possible for a train to pass from one track to another. Hundreds of other patents attracted engineers, designers, machinists, pipe-fitters, tool-and-die specialists, boiler-makers, welders, electricians, foundrymen, patternmakers, and excellent European-trained apprentices.

The Albred family glanced broken-heartedly at the square, plain brick structure that would be their new home and business in Eastburgh. The dilapidated structure resembled a broken down fortress. It was built in front of the great high cement wall which supported the Pennsylvania Railroad tracks. The Union Railroad ran back and forth transporting employees to Edgar Thompson Steel Works in the metropolis of Braddock. History recorded that General Braddock led British and colonial troops in a disastrous expedition against Fort Duquesne during the French and Indian War in 1754. He was duly honored with a great gray stone statue in full regalia looking toward the steel plant's general office. In this town, the Albred family found a temporary apartment while they waited for the building to be repaired, cleaned and readied for their new business.

The pitiful looking brick building which would house the new hotel resembled part of the foregone disastrous expedition, some bygone remains of the war of 1754 fought nearby. Lizzie stared at the crooked wobbly, looking bricks losing mortar daily. It had not looked as broken down on the day she first visited it six months ago, or had her aspirations clouded her common sense?

Once again Lizzie had to enlist her imaginative energy to visualize the evolution of this structure, from a broken down wreck to a warm, bustling establishment teeming with guests. Once again she faced insurmountable odds, since even this was impossible for her to conjure. She and Zach stepped through the ruins of warped, shaky floor boards badly stained from a persistently leaky roof; two cracked split beams ready to give way with the next slight breeze and lots of debris, the remains of past attempts of habitation. A contractor they had brought along for repair estimates stood in a far corner taking notes, shaking his head simultaneously.

"Don't worry Liz, it can all be fixed. It might take a few years, but we will work hard at it. It will be all right." Zach said, kicking an old decayed shoe out of the way.

He knew from experience living with Lizzie that she would go through at least three stages: outrage, despair, and eventual reasoning. The last would lead to a plan for complete recovery. He would stand by ready for her last temperament change to come about because Zach knew his Lizzie could never be discouraged. Lizzie laid her face in her hands on the verge of tears.

"I have used up all our money to buy this building, never thinking we would have to make so many changes. Did you ever see such a mess? It will take a long time to restore it, even to a livable state. We'll have to try to get by on the small amount of money we have left."

Later, as they sat planning while having a cup of coffee in their tiny apartment, a messenger brought a large brown envelope to their door with an estimate of repairs. Lizzie threw her hands up in the air at the sight of the figures.

"This is too much money to fix the building and make it presentable for us. How can we have paying customers in this war- torn place?" She folded the paper, gazing forlornly into the folds as if an answer lay there. "We might as well build a brand new building."

She pulled herself up on an old, reliable, high wooden stool nearby. One of the sturdy fixtures, which had been behind the counter of their old store. In her weakness of defeat, Lizzie would go to the only place she knew for spiritual guidance to contemplate the next move. It seemed that she was so close and, yet, the barriers were there, keeping her away from the plan she had tried to set in to motion.

"You have helped me so many times in the years since, I left my homeland, Dear Lord. Here I am, asking you again for a favor."

Her prayerful whispers sibilated throughout the dark, silent church, while the candle flame illuminated a sculptured form of Jesus. His red pupils had been painted by some artist probably wanting their exaggeration reflected from the back of the church. A long, loose-fitting red and white garment revealed one bare foot stepping out to match his outstretched hands reaching out to help anyone who interceded. This was her first visit to St. Thomas Church, and there was an adage in the faith that one could make three wishes upon entering a new church. Looking around at the fourteen stations of the cross, she made three wishes promising God, once again, "I will help to prepare my son to carry on your work if you will please help me find a way to turn this building into a hotel."

There. She had bargained with God and, like Abraham, she offered him her precious son.

Zach knew about business loans like the Russell Sage Foundation started in 1906, that helped immigrants, but he was not sure how they could tap into the money supply. The florist shop where he had worked in Philadelphia had financed his business through the Uniform Small Business Loan Law adopted in Pennsylvania and New Jersey, the only states who would loan money without security. Walking the streets of Eastburgh that afternoon, he went from bank to bank relating his problem.

"Why not go to the Carnegie Foundation and ask for funds." Stated Mr. Hovanec, a kindly man from The Mellon Bank. "Apply for funds under the auspices that you will be providing room and board for their employees. Here, let's sit down and write a letter together, then I'll call Mr. Carmichael, the Manager, in Pittsburgh. He'll know what to do. Leave everything to me."

Zach could hardly wait to get back to the apartment

that evening to tell Lizzie their good fortune.

"They'll give us three hundred dollars, enough to get started, until we start making money on our own."

Lizzie ran into her husband's arms, joyfully thanking God for this man who shared her thoughts and dreams. Life was wonderful and, once again on the right track. They could go forward to the next step of remodeling the building that would become their hotel.

Who was that out in the hall making confusion at this hour of the morning? She Shuffled down the hallway through the darkness at three o'clock,

"It's probably that no-account Shaughnessy, always the last one to leave the bar," Lizzie muttered.

Creeping out of the room throwing her flannel robe over her nightgown as she fled, she left Zach snoring loudly through his wiry-white whiskers. Due to the day's events, she had lain there for sometime unable to sleep that night, turning over and over again the dreaded news Aggie had reported. Stealing down to the last step she raised the iron plate. She could see him bent over at the dim reading lamp table where they usually kept old menus, price lists and messages for guests. Suddenly the intruder looked up and Lizzie raised her weapon.

"Hi Mom."

They held each other in an embrace.

"Johnny, my son, you're home. Did you hitch a ride instead of taking the train? You bad boy, taking a chance like that, what are we going to do with you!"

"One at a time, Ma, I got a ride most of the way home and then hitchhiked the rest of the way. Some nice guy picked me up.

Knowing they would broach the subject uppermost on their minds, they languished in their hearty greeting strolling arm in arm to the large, limitless coffee urn always ready in the corner of the commodious kitchen.

Chapter 6 Deception

In the American culture, parental authority was generally respected as law and control over families. Immigrants entered mainstream society, and raised their children between two different cultural worlds. Blaming themselves for their mistakes in parenting rarely happened, much less admitting their indiscretions to their children. These type of parents often felt that the acknowledgment of their failings loosened control over their children, subsequently lowering the effect of the parental authoritative role.

In this context, Lizzie made all of the decisions for her family, never asking their opinions, particularly where they were concerned. One time, and one time only this past summer, Johnny had tried to approach his mother about his aspirations.

"Mom, there are so many choices of curriculum at school. I'm not sure if being a priest is what I want to do. Maybe I can take some other courses, like animal husbandry, or political science." Without delay, Lizzie interjected.

"No, no, God has wanted you from the beginning, Johnny, not many people can do His work. But you are a natural to guide His Flock."

It was almost as if she were making a public announcement, or a recording, talking to the wall, as if he didn't exist.

She had never been a conventional Mother. Both she and Zach performed nontraditional roles as parents. Lizzie had always preached, "Don't do as I do, do as I say." Therefore, how could their family be expected to conform to any traditional pattern?

Whichever one of these philosophies manifested itself within Lizzie, inherently she had worked to empower Johnny from birth, instilling in him, his prominent role in life. A major part of her lived through Johnny. "A male child can do all the things I'd only dreamed of doing and never felt I could do, being a woman, particularly as an official in the Catholic church." He was predestined to be her route into that secret domain.

One of the important events Lizzie had not counted on was Johnny's removal from her authority to the jurisdiction of the Benedictines who gave him room to make choices. Also being removed from her, he began to see her as a woman in the world, a powerful woman who could take control of any situation and change it to her liking. He had never revolted against her wishes for him since they had become a way of life. Now a senior in college, he had grown into his "own man." His affection for her did not diminish as far as he was concerned, but her control over his life had ended.

"You're what?" Since when you make the rules around here? Where will you live, and what will you live on? What kind of a hussy is this Gesner girl, robbing God of a man of the church?" Johnny knew his mother was extremely upset when she lapsed into broken English, the emotional upheaval intercepting her proper word usage. He knew it would be difficult, and he was right on target. Flaming intense hazel eyes blazed with furious denial, as she pounded her strong fists with threats of his banishment.

"I have spent thousands to get you established. Well, you'll never see a penny of my money again, and don't ever bring that woman around here, Mister." She began flailing and waving her strong arms, all the time pointing at him, similar to a "fire and brimstone" preacher conducting a lively Sunday gospel service.

But hardest of all for him to watch, was her final

collapse into tearful despair, holding her dust-cap clad head in her hands, and looking older than her forty years. "Oh, why are you doing this to me?" She sobbed, tears and sweat streaming down through the lines in her face, carrying with them a smudge of dirt she'd picked up somewhere cleaning that morning.

"I raised you from a baby—worked my hands to the bone doing it—and what do I get for it? You let yourself be vulnerable to the ways of the flesh. Oh Johnny, you could be a Bishop or Cardinal even, in the hierarchy of the church. People throwing themselves at your feet, God's messenger. Why did you become so weak, how could you fall for an ordinary girl like this?"

Johnny resented her last line but knew, as she looked into his eyes, that she might be weakening. And as bad as he felt, he had to stay his ground on this one. He sat as still as he could, trying to emulate the way his father withstood so many of her outbursts. But this one surpassed them all. Her ship had sunk as well. She felt miserable, as if she was going down with him into the abyss of hell and damnation, all hopes and dreams buried forever. A lifetime of nurturing Johnny toward the most wonderful calling a man could hope for ended in a careless romance with someone she never wanted to meet.

Later in the darkened room, with only the desk lamp illuminating her sad face, as she sat gaping into the roll-top desk, devoid of human feeling and drained of the desire to live, the door behind her creaked open as Zach pushed open the dark door. Settling his large form into the nearby leather chair, he looked imploringly into her despondent eyes.

"My dear Lizzie, John is a man who must make his own way in the world, you cannot command his life anymore. He has found love with this woman and you must accept it or he will go away for good. And I don't think you want him to do that. You've got to stop running his life now.

Besides, Dell is a nice Hungarian Catholic girl. What more can you ask?"

He smiled compassionately into her eyes, stretching his long arm around her small, pudgy frame. His gentleness brought forth a new flow of sorrowful tears from her already red, puffy eyes, but with the flow of recognition came resentment, as she listened to his words.

Zach had a way of seeing good things come from every new situation. He's such an optimistic man, too bad I don't listen to him more often, Lizzie thought. Maybe she would not have gone through with some of her unworthy ideas, some of which led her having to face moments like these. But no, she probably would never have been talked out of the life she had wished for her Johnny. The reflection brought another tear to her eye. Her dream of her son, the priest, walking into the hotel in front of all the patrons commanding a hierarchy had died. She thought for one split moment of stepping in the middle of John and Dell's relationship, going to see her family, forcing them to see things her way and explaining the fact that she couldn't get in the way of his aspirations. No, Zach was right. It would only drive them further away and she did love her son. Why not go along with the wedding, and then make them suffer with their mistake? They would eventually come to their senses. Yes, she would follow a different strategy, pretending she was happy about the turn of events. The time would come when they would regret their decision to go against God.

In the meantime, she would go through the motions of planning a wedding, buying the wedding dress and planning a banquet fit for royalty. Though Lizzie knew in the back of her mind, she may be once again rushing in the wrong door, she had to redeem herself with Johnny. And she had to get excited about something. The whole charade might be fun and she really didn't trust anyone else to take on this task, especially her children. For one instant, she stopped to think about why she mistrusted them in that way. Had she actually run all of their lives along with the hotel routine? If only she could begin to believe in her family. But there were too many distractions in this society forcing them to go astray. Material things out there, people doing anything for the sake of money. Lots of people had even stopped going to church, worshipping the almighty dollar instead.

She had heard stories, for instance, about Phil being involved with that bootleggin' gang from Rankin, but she refused to believe them. Why would he want more money? He had all he needed. She had even looked away when he'd helped himself to a ten or twenty from the cash register, having written it off to overhead on business. She had also overlooked the price tags on clothes Aggie had brought home from Sach's. Twenty five dollars for just one beaded dress. They only handled cash. Lizzie did not believe in checks or depositing her money in any of the local banks. Mismanagement had always prevailed in the local banks, depositors' money continually being lost, especially when the big conglomerates like the Mellon family, took over. Now, the United States Congress had passed the bank acts trying to guarantee U.S. bonds and provide circulation, but she knew some neighborhood businessmen who'd recently lost money through a bank failure and still would not take chances on someone handling her money. She and Zach had a small steel, fireproof safe hidden under their bed where their business papers were also kept with the cash taken in at the end of the day. Nevertheless she patted the lump in her stocking where two $500 bills were safely rolled into the elastic garter. That was the safest bank she knew.

"Picture you upon my knee, just two for tea, and tea for two, me for you and you for me alone."

They sat by the upright playing and singing together most evenings, now that he had returned from school for good. Sometimes Johnny would whistle while Dell played the melody. Everything was in tune these days as they whirled through a brusque courtship. They would be married at the end of January. Wedding plans were evolving into an enormous undertaking, which would include most of the townspeople. Dell was not sure that she wanted the big ceremony John's mother had mentioned to him, but it would be the beginning of the wonderful life she would share with John and she was happier than she had ever been in her whole life. Johnny had come to her house with her Christmas present.

"Dell, I want you to marry me and the sooner the better." He had blurted it out right there in the hallway upon seeing her the first time since last summer. She was breathless. Throwing her delicate arms around his husky frame revealed her eager response. Mom and Pop were astonished at the spontaneity displayed by this twosome who hadn't even given one thought to any future plans. That would never be done in this manner in their day. In Europe, marriages were planned between families years in advance. The woman had a dowry, maybe some land and livestock. And the courtship usually involved the couple taking family members along for afternoon get-togethers, known as dates in America. But in this country they found relationships started with an attraction toward each other, growing into strong loving feelings leading to marriage. The entire incident seemed like a fairly tale based on flimsy feelings not to be trusted.

"I think I'll work at the hotel for a while, until I can decide what my future will be." Johnny promised Dell's Father, so that he would not worry about the financial welfare of his daughter.

Pop was skeptical regarding Johnny's position in the contentious hotel mood, but he said nothing. He'd heard about the exploits of the son and daughter of Lizzie Albred. She was a tough business manager, but her son and daughter had free reign with plenty of money in their pockets to get themselves into trouble. The thought of his daughter living there among these two made him feel a little wary. He hoped she wouldn't become mistreated as part of the help, drudging from morning until night, working the same hours as Lizzie herself seemed to do. Putting his thoughts to rest, he took assurance in the fact that Johnny would take care of his new wife and family. And wasn't Lizzie a religious person with good fundamental values spending most mornings at mass? He didn't know Zach as well, only that he was a tall, quiet man who followed his wife's leadership and supported her in the business.

Well, maybe they would not have children right away, then they could make some plans. He wished they would at least wait for a little while to get married. So impatient, he could not see the rush, but then he realized their passions were not to be put off any longer. He didn't mention any of these thoughts to Mom, she was just as enraptured as Dell about the new love and marriage flourishing. These romantic ideas, nurtured mostly by women, didn't interest him. He was a practical man—he knew how fast the icing disappeared on the cake. Beautiful weddings turning into miserable lives. Everything looks nice before you get to know what's behind the door. He had learned all about fancy covers from advertising his garage.

In Europe, it was not all for show. The attention was on the mechanic and what he knew about motors. He came out of trade school in Saxonburg knowing how machinery was put together from beginning to end. He could build his own car if he chose. But here in America, people wanted to be entertained before they bought something. They actually believed these announcements, even if they weren't honest. "Fill the people's mind with product propaganda," the radio sponsors had told him. His simple slogan, "Pop's popular Maxwells," would no longer sell cars. A good motor under the hood was no longer good enough. A fancy dashboard had to be mentioned, mirrors, mirrors everywhere. And now chrome was in fashion. He was not sure whether he could play these big publicity games. That was why Johnny was such a good salesman for his garage. He could bullshit, Pop pondered, God could he bullshit those customers.

"This bright shiny coupe's made especially for you," he would dazzle them. "Look at that fancy chrome cigarette lighter right at your disposal on the dashboard."

He would make it all a personal experience from the time they walked into the garage, remembering the customers by name. He knew them all or would find them out in a split second by mentioning a mother or an uncle. He guessed that deep down inside the true reason he might not trust him with Dell's life, was because Johnny could run a line from here to Detroit. Dell was such a naive young woman who loved life and trusted people. Hopefully Johnny loved her for that reason. Lizzie had so much control over him. Would she now dominate them both?

Pop could still remember Dell's first day of school when she came home crying.

"Sister made me stay in the cloakroom because I didn't know the English names of things."

First, he was mad at the nuns, then at his wife for speaking Hungarian all the time at home, even singing in old country. What was wrong with that woman?

"Mother, I hope she's not going to prance around here like some princess just because she's marrying your favorite son," Aggie quipped, lifting the pink taffeta bridesmaid dress over her ample bosom, adjusting it accordingly as it fell down in voluminous folds along her full body. She and Lizzie had gone out that afternoon to purchase all of her wedding clothes, including bridal gown, veil, white shoes, stockings and underwear for Dell.

The new couple would be surprised and dissuaded, when they were actually confronted over the holidays. Lizzie was almost certain these symbols of marriage would discourage their planning. She knew they'd gone a little too far with their purchases, but Aggie was having such a good time with it. Johnny had also hinted to her, "Mom, Pop's garage isn't doing that well since Jack Phillips put up a swanky new four car showroom down the street. I think the competition is a little stiff for him." Lizzie took all this to mean the Gesner's couldn't afford a wedding anyway even if Johnny and Dell would really get married. She was even going through the motions of calling Father O'Flaherty to schedule high mass at 10:00 a.m. on January 27th. At least someone would take care to run the whole affair correctly since most of the people in Eastburgh would be invited. If the Gesner's objected she would just have to stand her ground. "We are business people, we know how to arrange these social events, and that is that!" If nothing else, they would benefit from the gathering of people, promoting business at the hotel.

Lizzie hoped the wedding gown they'd chosen would not be too big for the scrawny-shaped Dell, who didn't even look like she weighed one hundred pounds. Passing up the more decorative sequined and beaded gowns, she bought, instead, a plain tulle mid-calf length informal style lending an informal look to the entire wedding party. For her head, a bouffant veil with a band of seed pearls and sequins. The latest in bridal wear, the clerk had said. She'd also sold them long opera gloves to complete the look. She didn't think the

Gesner's would mind them going ahead to prepare for all the wedding essentials—somehow she knew they wouldn't know how to go about buying the right accessories anyway. Mrs. Gesner was mostly confined to her home, a timid withdrawn woman. Although, Lizzie had heard she had a beautiful voice, and sang lovely Hungarian songs for small social get-togethers. Therefore, she assumed that their doing the difficult chore of bringing all the desired necessities together for this event would be appreciated. It didn't even occur to her to consult with any of them in her plans for the function. Besides, it would probably be canceled anyway when Johnny and Dell realized what they were really getting into. This way they would be spared the ordeal of getting ready for the imaginary day. And, even though she more than anyone was gravely disappointed, she would not have the occasion turned into a debauchery.

Aggie was pleased with her image in the long mirror in her bedroom, as she stepped around from side to side in various poses.

"Well, at least I'll look stylish, but I'm not so sure about that plain thing I told Mom to buy for the bride. It'll probably just hang on her like a drape over a coat hanger. I really can not believe Johnny is marrying that bony thing. Her, sister Mary, will just love that shapeless dress we picked out for her to wear as Matron of Honor. That position should be mine, I hate being just a bridesmaid. Hmm," she thought as she pulled in the filmy material at her waist. "I understand Mary has a nice figure, maybe I should take a few tucks in here and there. She won't show me up."

She was glad that she'd suggested to her mother that they go ahead and plan, even to the point of buying everybody's wedding clothes for the big day.

"They will all be so pleased, Mom, this way they won't have to do anything on such short notice," she smiled knowingly that she'd convinced her mother.

The Gesner's were so "old country," what kind of taste could they have for a formal wedding of this class? Besides, Mom had plenty of money and they could have the reception right here in the hotel. Wouldn't they be taking up housekeeping here, too? Ha, that was a joke! "Ha Ha," Aggie laughed. The laugh was on Johnny. With all his education, he would end up right here in the same old hotel with the rest of us. Most of us are trying to get out of this dirty old factory town, like myself for instance, everyone knows I was destined for something better. I was meant to have been born into royalty, weighted down with diamonds and jewels of every variety. She sat on the edge of her blue chenille bedspread stretching her short dimply knees out in front of her, gracefully walking across the length of her bedroom always within complete view of the huge oval bureau mirror. God knows I have queenly qualities. Yes, she would keep her eye on Johnny's new wife who might try to steal the attention away from her. She better keep her nose to the grindstone along with everyone else, the little princess. With this she swung her satin shoe, giggled and rolled over for a nap. There'd be no hotel work for her today.

Holding on to fumbling fingers and hands as they slid down the icy path to the Rivoli Theater, proved to be quite a conquest as John and Dell struggled to keep their balance that wintry Sunday evening. Freezing rain and snow had settled over the city all day, but had not dampened their plans to see the new Marx Brothers movie, Animal Crackers, opening today.

"Whoa, John," Dell yelled, as she tumbled down on to her right side, feet flying high up in the air. As he reached for her too late, Johnny slid into her and they doubled up into rolling laughter. It wasn't the first time she had almost peed her pants laughing with her soon-to-be husband. The two of them really had fun together—their harmony was better than she could ever have dreamed. John was always making everybody laugh. Just when everything seemed quiet at her house, he would come into the room dressed up in Mom's clothes, as they all held their sides laughing at his antics. She wished to eventually share his sense of humor of laughing at life.

She had always been so serious, most of her family took life serious. They could even be morbid sometime. Johnny would be good for them.

As part of the academic world for ten long years, Johnny had acquired extensive discipline in literature, often quoting Shakespearean verse to demonstrate his feelings about the extensive consumerism and secularism he thought eroded the pureness of spirit within a person, which had been part of his spiritual training. Eloquently vocalizing, sometime down on his knees he would recite, *All the world's a stage, And the men and women merely players. They have their exits and their entrances; And one man in his time plays many parts.*

Dell thought he might be an actor at heart, but knew his spiritual philosophy of their short life on earth probably originated at the seminary. As human beings, they were here acting parts out and their spirit would go on for all eternity. Johnny spent much of his time attacking the evils of capitalism, concerned that people were too involved with material possessions.

Dell would sometime be overwhelmed by his intelligence.

"John, it's because of me that you are leaving college, do you think you should continue your education, perhaps in a different course of study?" Dell would inquire, feeling responsible for his decision. But he would always quell her apprehension.

"Dell, my primary purpose for being there was to be a priest. It would be hard to turn these courses of study into something else, except to teach and I'm not interested in that vocation right now."

Their love was first, but she wondered what direction their future together would take.

She would be giving notice at her office two weeks before her wedding since company policy dictated that women could not continue to work after marriage. Dell wondered why it was that all the married men continued to work? It was just another standard rule for women only, that she could not understand. It seemed companies did not want women to get ahead. Most of the women she knew kept their marriages a secret just to keep their jobs. This dishonesty upset her, because only two weeks ago she had been promoted to secretary to the Supervisor of Marketing, picked especially for her outstanding performance by an accomplished Business Director. It was a strange, ambiguous feeling; she had devoted a lot of care and attention to having a good career, yet she was also thrilled to be marrying this wonderful man. Deep inside she was torn by this decision. She would miss the people she worked with—they had become one big happy family. She had to look ahead to her own family. She and John both loved children and wanted at least, "A boy for you and a girl for me, can't you see how happy we will be." They had sang the words of Tea For Two, looking into each other's eyes.

Mary was angry.

"Those coarse, ignorant people. How could they? Just going out like that buying all of our clothes for the wedding! I can't believe it, Mom, even the wedding dress for Dell. And I also can't believe Dell is taking it so calmly!"

"I suppose Mrs. Albred has the money to spend,"

Theresa reasoned for her distraught daughter, thinking that maybe she knows Pop has not been selling as many cars as before.

"Wedding's do cost money these days. I was planning to sew a dress for Dell from a pattern already cut out from one of her other dresses. I had already ordered a good grade of white percale. Then I would crochet a trim around the hem, sleeves and neckline later," Theresa replied with downcast eyes, having begun to realize how her plans were usurped by the swiftly acting Lizzie.

Mary felt the hurt in her mother's watering blue eyes and vowed to have a word with Lizzie and her "prima donna" daughter the next day after work. Why were these people so forceful? It was the same old story, money talked. Well, she would do something about their "wedding plans" tomorrow.

What a smelly place, Mary thought. Who would want to spend their life in a place like this? The acrid blend of liquor, smoke, cabbage, cleaning fluids and human sweat simultaneously reached her senses as she found herself inside the Albred Hotel. Tripping over a shiny brass spittoon, she looked up to recognize Zach, greeting her with his wide handlebar mustache opening into a big smile.

"You're the Gesner girl, aren't you? Make yourself at home. What can I bring you from the bar, did you have dinner yet?" He questioned accommodatingly, immediately putting her initial fears to rest. What a nice man, very much like Johnny, she thought, waiting for Lizzie to appear. A smiling young woman emerged out of nowhere graciously setting a full plate of steaming stuffed cabbage before her. I wonder if they know I did not come here to eat.

"Hello, Mary," came the words from the dark wooded doorway, long before the large white-aproned Lizzie herself surfaced. "Are you comfortable, how is the food? What will you have to drink? Where is your bread and butter? Annie!" she shouted, as the young girl nervously ran for the rest of the table settings.

Observing the busy restaurant world movement around her, Mary began to comprehend where the Albred's aggressive and contentious behavior originated. In an active business such as this one could not prosper with indecisive people around who took each day as it came along. Hard working industrious people with planning objectives made well in advance were the kind who built this kind of an establishment. Pondering, Mary found herself eating the delicious cabbage dish, wiping the plate clean with a large morsel of Lizzie's fresh homemade bread. Realizing what wonderful food she had eaten, she became angry that her temperament softened, making it more difficult to accomplish the mission she'd set out to do. They had all made her feel so much at home here—what nice people.

"Mom said you were out here. Hi, I'm Aggie, C'mon, I'll show you what we're gonna wear for the big day."

She jerked swiftly around scarcely looking at Mary, long auburn curls bounced with each step she took. What an old fashioned hair style, Mary thought, staring at the back of Aggie's springy coiffure as they walked through the dark oak paneled hallway and up the long creaky wooden staircase to Aggie's second floor bedroom. At first glance, she thought she'd stepped into a fashionable woman's store, having never seen so many clothes in a single room before. Most were thrown nonchalantly over chairs and dressing tables, as if a one-day-only sale was transpiring. Nearly tripping over a gold leather sandal lying in front of Aggie's unmade bed, she stooped to pick it up only to see dozens more shoes beside it under the bed, some still in boxes with brand new, price tags stuck to their soles. What kind of a person was Aggie to squander money on all these clothes? Remembering her mother whom she had just met downstairs, a countenance humbled by years of hard work standing before her, she could hardly believe this was her daughter living in the lap of luxury right here under the same roof.

"I hope you like these," Aggie blurted, tossing yesterday's blue cotton chemise from the foot of the bed, uncovering a shiny satin garment. "But it really doesn't matter 'cause they're all bought and paid by us!"

She held the silky fabric against her and paraded around the room, falling in love again with her reflected image. Watching from across the room, Mary was taken aback by her cutting words. She personally didn't know anyone as bold as this. Was it possible Aggie thought she was better than most people or was she just ignorant of how the other half lived in her own little world where she was so infatuated with herself? Worst of all, she had no idea the hurt her words caused falling on another's ears. This probably meant she was without any social conscience whatsoever.

"My mother is a wonderful seamstress. She was going to make all of our dresses for the wedding, well, at least the bride's."

There, it was out, she had told her they had plans of their own, that her family wouldn't let these Albred's run everything. Aggie's incredulous expression shot bullets through Mary.

"You know we are important people in this town, we can't be seen wearing some homemade unstylish rags put together by your mother!"

"But you don't know a thing about the beautiful clothes my mother sews, how can you say that?"

This last statement out, Mary turned her back on the insensitive, wicked woman, hoping this whole thing would go away. Making her way back to the door past a blurry

Mr. and Mrs. Albred, she could only pity poor Dell having to be related to a witch like that. And to think she would actually be living under the same roof. Running out of the square brick building, tears continued to stream down Mary's face until she reached the street, safely turning the corner toward her house. Painful frustration gripped her as she thought about telling Mom and Pop about this woman. It would be difficult to tell them, since they probably never encountered people of this nature. They were gentle people and probably wouldn't understand the crude and arrogant behavior some business people, like the Albreds, displayed. Aggie, on the other hand, was reaping the material rewards of her parents' years of hard work.

Her father had his car garage and dealt with many people everyday, but he never made millions. Lizzie and Zach came from the outlying farm villages in Europe, whereas Theresa and Pop had lived in the progressively cultural Budapest among students and business people. They were refined people who would not speak out of turn, much less insult someone openly, as Aggie had. Mary was saddened about the life her sweet, innocent sister would live, who never had an unkind thing to say about anyone. What a conceited girl, so in love with herself, she muttered. Still seething, she sat down on the steps outside her house. Hoping her Mother would not see her, she tried to calm down before opening the door. How could she ever take part in a wedding ceremony with that miserable creature strutting around as if she were on the Broadway stage? Well, she would just do her best to avoid her. Starting tomorrow she would even walk to work on the other side of the street, and pass the hotel quickly everyday. In some ways she felt bad for her behavior, running out on Johnny's mother and father like that. They did seem like nice people. How could they have raised a daughter and their son, Phil, too. She'd seen him walking out earlier. A rogue of a guy, who was one of the local guys trying to imitate Al Capone, always hanging around with those hoodlums. Everyone knew he brought boot-leg whisky into town, but the Feds never knew exactly where it was hidden. Those Albreds were even above government law. They probably paid off everyone in town. She was especially sorry for the day she encouraged Dell to meet Johnny in Pop's garage. Who would've thought it would lead to all this misery?

"Pa, who was that lady runnin' out o' here like that? She looked like someone gave 'er some o' that ole elderberry wine. Wha' happened?" Phil yelled excitedly to his father.

"I think that was the Gesner girl, son. Something must've happened up there with Aggie," he said, nodding toward the upstairs bedroom.

"I'm not surprised. Her highness is probably jealous of the sister of the bride, too. After all she is a looker," Phil replied.

"Guess I'm goin' to call your mother to patch this one up, what get's into that girl?" Zach said, petting his unruly bristled mustache.

"I'll tell ya what gets into 'er, she's stuck on herself, a spoiled brat, all she has to do is ask and it's hers!" Now Phil was shouting, bringing Lizzie running from the kitchen.

"What's the matter with you? The customers are watching," she said, in a low voice, a wisp of hair falling into a stream of sweat beads down her forehead.

"I can't help it Ma, she just said something to Dell's sister, Mary. Ya gotta do somethin' about that girl," he looked at his mother inquiringly.

Lizzie stood wiping red swollen hands on her already huge stained apron, the doubled waistband pulling away from her with the strain.

"I knew I should have had the family get-together dinner this week instead of next week, at least we could have all gotten to know each other already."

"There ya go again, makin' excuses again for that dumb dora upstairs," Phil mumbled, walking away. He knew there was only so much he could say to his mother without her turning on him.

"It's okay Liz, we'll have the dinner this week. We'll have the Gesner family down for a "Get Acquainted Party". We'll close the doors to all outside customers. We have to help the kids out by trying to get along," Zach placated.

"I tell you she is a she-devil!" Mary shouted to her sister. "She thinks she's better than anyone on this earth. Well, what do you think about her and her mother picking out your dress and veil, and everything else you'll wear on your wedding day? Isn't that being a little bold?"

Dell sat back relaxed against a cushion in a corner of the living room settee, thin legs crossed beneath her, very much removed from the anxiety Mary exhibited. She had just bought the F. Scott Fitzgerald best seller, *The Beautiful And The Damned*, and was engrossed with the intense story line.

"Aggie is having a good time getting ready for the wedding, I think you probably didn't get to know her. You'll see her at the dinner they're planning. Everybody is tense about all this, Mary. John's Mom always goes out of her way for these events, always helping everyone because that's the kind of person she is, and what's more, she has the money to do it whenever she wants. What a generous person. Do you know she has most of the poor people lined up at the back door for food at the end of the day? Usually they come into the restaurant begging for change, but instead she gives them a free meal. Isn't that something? I think she takes care of most of the people of Eastburg.

Mary stared at her in disbelief. She couldn't believe her ears. Dell was on some other planet, removed from the reality of what she would wear at her own wedding, which in her mind, should be the uppermost desire in any woman's lifetime.

"You know, John and I just want to have our religious ceremony with everyone at the church as witnesses. We really don't care what we wear to the ceremony. Mary, don't worry, just think about all the money Mom and Pop are saving. Mrs. Albred knows how to take care of everything. She cooks and manages that big restaurant with all the people who work there and also makes the hotel comfortable for the new people living there as their first home in America. Johnny told me yesterday about Milos Yankovic's wife having some blood disease over in the old country. She wasn't expected to live much longer. Mrs. Albred gave him the money to bring her over here so she could get medical treatment."

Mary sat listening and thinking maybe she had been a little too hasty.

"Alright, so maybe she is a charitable woman, but I think she has been a little too good to her little girl."

She'd tried but still couldn't hide her bitter resentment toward Aggie. They had gotten off to a bad start in their family relations and would probably remain that way for a long time. Dell just didn't care about the same things as she, it had always been this way. One example was her personal appearance. The hems on Dell's dresses never hung straight and most of the time her silk stockings bagged on her shapeless legs. Mary couldn't believe she showed up for work looking that way. So in the long run, her sister's attitude didn't surprise her. On the inside, Dell was a good person. Once again she got the chills when she thought about her going to live there.

Later that evening as Lizzie and Aggie were getting the good china down from the huge cupboard, Lizzie inquired about what had happened earlier in the day.

"Mary said she hated the wedding clothes and ran out for no reason at all," Aggie lied. "I hope she doesn't come around much after the wedding."

Lizzie handed her the large meat platter.

"You have to get along with your brother's new family. Not one of us are happy about this but we have to accept it."

Lizzie constantly worried about Aggie's mental state . She had contracted scarlet fever before she was two years old and had gone into convulsions from an infection in her middle ear while Lizzie had been at the freight yard buying fruit and vegetables for their store in Wilkes Barre. She had left her with one of the cleaning women and never forgave herself for not being with her young child while she lay suffering. The guilt of that horrible time still held its effect on her, especially since she had not taken Aggie for tests later which might have proven whether she suffered from brain damage during the ordeal and could have been treated. The experience had prompted her to act indulgently toward Aggie, whatever her whims were, when she should have stood firm. Thank God her general health had been restored toward the end of that terrible year, allowing her to grow up to be a beautiful, strong young woman. But deep down inside Lizzie knew something was not exactly right with her daughter's reasoning powers and sincerely hoped some nice young man would marry her.

Pulling the wooden potato peeler handle toward her, she gazed at the long continuous flow of brown knobby peels falling into the deep sink, reflecting on her unsuccessful vocation of motherhood. She had not done well in her relationship with her children, especially with Johnny. There just wasn't enough time to do everything necessary for them and run the business. Probably some of the best moments of her life had slipped away. While she kneaded the huge ball of dough for the twenty loaves of bread to be baked the next morning, two women pushing baby carriages past the hotel kitchen window reminded her it was too late to recall some of the important occasions she had missed. The burden of parenting often fell into the hands of Johnny. She could hear him disciplining his younger sister and brother from the backroom while she poured over the hotel accounts for that month. He was such a responsible little boy.

"No you cannot cross the street, the streetcars run too fast in front of our place, you might get hit. Phil, do you remember when the milkman's horse stampeded last week?"

Reaching down for her apron corner, she wiped a tear from the corner of her eye. What would she ever have done without him and his good judgment? Now this little boy was getting married, after all the plans she had made for him. What direction would his life take now? He had no choice but to learn the inside of the hotel and restaurant business.

Because most of the food from eastern Europe had deep cultural roots, it could not be consumed by just anyone not having an understanding of the heritage therein. At least this was the philosophy Lizzie employed, lowering herself into the spindle-back desk chair behind the huge desk to write a list of foods to be purchased for the pending event. This would be the most special feast she had ever prepared. And, even though she had to put aside her true feelings, she began to plan a banquet that would celebrate life, laughter, conversation and friendship gathered together with their two families. She would think of it as a religious experience, a Benediction where she would reign in offering distinctive hereditary culinary delights whose origins brought back reminiscences their families left far behind in Europe. Maybe a mother kneeling to weed in her garden that brought forth the precious vegetables used or an important event where the food was last served. The sour mushroom soup reminded her of regular occurrence when, as a child, she and her Father rose very early in the morning to pick wild mushrooms in the dense woods.

"No, not that one," he would say in his deep authoritative voice. "That one is a toadstool."

Eventually, she knew which plant to pick on sight. Later, Papa would thread them on a string to hang up to dry out for the soup Mama would cook.

A rush of excitement stirred within her as she envisioned the delighted faces of the two families while she brought forth her handiwork from the kitchen. She would work all through the night before plying the pirohy dough made with fresh butter from the nearest farm. Spreading the sweetened cottage cheese, mashed potato and cabbage fillings over each individual triangle, then frying each with buttered bread crumbs required at least a half day's time. But this delicacy would only be a side dish to the nearby roaster of beef gulyaś simmering, sending mouth-watering vapors throughout the hotel and signaling boarders of the approaching feast. Delighting in everything she did in the kitchen, the hurt she had felt the month before began to heal into an ugly scar that would remain forever.

Most of the Gesner's came from Debrecen, Hungary, however Pop's Father had been an Engineering Professor at the Technical University of Dresden near Saxony in Germany. The Gesner family was different from them in many ways; they were a gentle and thoughtful people. Pop ran his business with a low profile, not with the outburst of emotion the Albreds exuded in their everyday relations at the hotel. Lizzie had heard that Dell's mother, Theresa Voivida was raised near the capital of Budapest. She had seen her in church on Sundays with Pop. A tall, poised woman with long thick black hair pulled up around her head in a loose braid, she was known about town for her beautiful voice. A product of cultural refinement, she sang difficult Hungarian songs at various occasions. It was also rumored that she was not always treated with respect by her husband. Lizzie knew many women who feared their husbands. In some ways she had to blame them. Lizzie personally felt that all rights came to individuals upon their own demands. Just because they were beginning to vote, did not meant that they would be independent.

Laws certainly did not change people's ways of life. Women had to begin to exercise control in other aspects of their life. It was all in the way she carried herself and her attitude. Even as Lizzie was growing up, she knew women who were punished like small children for any reason, especially if things went wrong in their husband's working day, like loss of a job or money problems. Many babies were conceived from forced sex during a drunken binge. There was no love or affection, or even respect in such a relationship since most were family-planned marriages. The Gesner's had such a marriage. Theresa was a humble woman who did not speak up to Pop, but kept her submissive role. And even though Lizzie had controlled her own life, she had sympathy for the women who were led around by some headstrong man. Once or twice she witnessed some husband flaunting his authority over his wife in her restaurant. She would step in with, "We know you're the boss, now go on and pick on someone your own size. Don't be bullying your Mrs. here." She knew they wouldn't sass her back because she would quickly throw them and their old cardboard suitcases out on the street.

Walking into dangerous situations never bothered Lizzie. She had once walked into the middle of fisticuffs between two huge, angry Magyar men in the back of the hotel. They had stepped outside after drinking most of the night, to settle their dispute. She knew they could just push her out of the way and continue their useless match, but she stepped into the middle, yanking and pulling their soiled long underwear with all her might scolding them like two bad boys.

"What would your poor mother say over there in Pecs, if she saw you two? She raised you both to be good boys. Your sisters are depending on you to make something of yourselves."

Finally, her matronly reasoning broke through their anger as they lowered their raging fists. Zach watched from the door, chastising himself for letting these two volatile Magyars drink so long without eating.

Chapter 7 Contemplation

"Thus a man and woman, who by the marriage covenant of conjugal love are no longer two, but one flesh, render mutual help and service to each other through an intimate union of their persons and of their actions. Through this union they experience the meaning of their oneness and attain to it with growing perfection day by day."

Matthew, Chapter 19:6

The stirring of passion Johnny felt for Dell was much different than those of the spiritual magnitude expressed for his Divine Redeemer developed in the teachings of the Benedictine Monks in his adolescent prep-school years at St. Vincent. As he grew, he began to sort out the kinds of love he should expect in his life. The spiritual love he had experienced earlier remained in the background now, as his body came alive with physical pleasure at the thought of Dell's trim, lithe body next to his in bed. He felt a thunderbolt of blood rush up at the mere thought of touching her smooth skin with his fingertips, knowing they would be intimate in one month on their wedding night. To this date they had tried to discipline their actions. Dell was much better at this than he, as she strictly defied any strong movements on his part for real intimacy. Once, when they were embracing on her living room settee all alone in the house, he felt her heart beating against him; determination urged him to go further to find the deeper warmth of her breast. But, looking up he caught her dark eyes quickening with fear and immediately halted his movement. The emotional frustration was extremely difficult for him and the source of passion and desire always left him feeling disconsolate. Some part of him wondered if some of the mystery of this relationship was the sexual challenge as well, to once and for all have a good roll in the hay with this chaste woman. But he quickly put these feelings aside because he knew other women who exhibited a pretentiousness that Dell didn't. She had some unreachable spirit he loved. Lately it had even crossed his mind that she, being virginal, was closer to God than he had ever been, telling him several times, especially after their relentless kisses and holding each other.

"Now, John, we are going to wait until our wedding is blessed in Holy Matrimony, aren't we?" she would say. "You stay over there, and let me get us some tea."

He wondered how she could be so cool with her innocent naive manner, but he usually complied, knowing she had an honest control in the situation which he respected. Realizing she sometimes showed an indifference which might be misread as inattentive to anyone else, he perceived her actions to be an avoidance to confront unpleasantries, like discussing what it would be like to move into the hotel with his family. She would say, "It sounds fine John, as long as we have our separate rooms to live as we please." But then she would look away troubled, as if into another distant world. He knew she had many unanswered questions, if just that they would have to walk to the end of the long hallway to share bathroom facilities with the other boarders and probably eat most of their meals in the big kitchen with them and his mother. Even though he knew his mother meant well, she might be intimidating to his young bride fresh from her protective home. He felt an overwhelming feeling of consternation, but, try as he may, he could not get her to express any displeasure openly. The first consciousness of love in their relationship, the giddy, happy phase when even the worst things in life appeared nonchalant had passed. Now the realities had begun to creep into view. After all, Dell had led a sheltered life, with a strong father in Pop, who watched over his daughter's lives constantly, insisting that they both have a higher education than the eighth grade which was all the state of Pennsylvania required in 1920. Dell had more education with her stenographic night school classes at Valley Creek than most of the women in their town.

For the first time in their relationship, he began to think about how their marriage would affect her well-being. Moving in at the hotel would probably present difficult problems for them both. He certainly was not going to have it easy working directly for his mother, he thought as he sat in the hotel office. The place he once thought was the most exciting spot in the world began to harbor a rank, sauerkraut smell. Studying employee records, he spent most of the day trying to become familiar with the housekeeping staff and some of their key suppliers. He found it interesting that none of his heretofore instruction would help him run this enterprise with its immigrants and Lizzie's homespun created atmosphere. That one accounting elective he'd taken at St. Vincent's could never begin to be applied to his mother's improvised system. She had spent years incorporating a makeshift procedure for debits and credits, that only she could comprehend, much less a mistrodden prodigal son trying to find out what made the business tick. Searching the big ledger for a method to the madness, his eyes focused on a small object deep in the corner of a pigeonhole in the back of the disorganized roll-top desk. Picking up the round little glass snow scene, he shook it vigorously, starting a tiny blizzard flying over the boy in a red snowsuit. The little lonely waif could have been him alone out in the cold, whose mother wasn't anywhere visible. A child made responsible before his time, taking on adult tasks, like counting large bills out at the end of the day. And if they didn't add up, he would face the wrath of his mother. Somehow she couldn't see past the profits into his child's anxious eyes, eager to have a boyhood of carefree fun. Watching at the large display window past the neatly stacked canned goods, he wondered what it would be like to climb the long hill and sled ride down. Guiding the American Flyer over the special trail of "boy-made" mounds of snow, with the sharp wind biting at his face, and reaching the bottom to tell of the new triumph. He'd never really had a childhood and deep within him loomed the controlling figure of his mother. Why had she governed his fate so rigidly? He wondered how long he had harbored this resentfulness that now surfaced clearly in front of him. Maybe it was always there, but somewhere along the way she'd made him feel that he was living his own life, making his own decisions, but he wasn't. He hadn't made one single choice in life without her being in on it. Were all mothers as possessive as this?

His father did the physical work in those days, unloading flour sacks and pickle barrels on to the wooden dollies to bring into the store. Usually the physical labor got the better of him as his breathing became labored. He sometimes wondered how his father handled the smoke-alcohol fumes around the bar filling his lungs now. But he seemed to know his limit, and would take his rest periods in between times.

Footsteps creaked on the hardwood floor behind him, jerking Johnny back to the present time.

"Did you make those checks out John, it's the end of the month and we don't want to fall behind!" Lizzie instructed.

"Yeah, Ma, but I'm trying to match the orders up with the billing, maybe I should do an inventory today," he said.

She turned around before walking back out,

"No, just follow orders, we have plenty of flour and the egg man just left several cartons."

It was hopeless, he thought. Any suggestion on how

to run this business was rebuffed. Nevertheless, I'll have to stay in this miserable condition until I find a career plan.

He prayed to God that she wouldn't continually bring up her regrets about him leaving the seminary. Just the other day they were pouring over the account for a new distributor for the hotel's dairy products.

"Ma, are you sure you wouldn't get a better deal if you got the butter and cottage cheese in bigger cases? You could buy a bigger ice box," he suggested.

"I've been buying this same amount for years," she said abruptly. "It would be throwing more money out the window at the beginning of the month. You don't know how I do things here, just watch now, don't give me any advice. Besides, you have been in another place, maybe that was the place for you."

He gritted his teeth, disgusted with what he was going to have to put up with after he was married later this month, this domineering woman who thought she knew it all.

Sometimes he would relieve his Dad at the bar when he took his afternoon and evening breaks. He was a lot easier to deal with everyday, but it was also clear that he was not in charge of the operation, especially after he'd said "Ask your mother," a few times when John wanted to install a hidden beer tap under the bar. Most people felt that the U.S. Congress would soon repeal prohibition and an Amendment was certainly on its way to become a law in government. These thoughts spurred Johnny to get the hotel bar ready for an upswing in business. He knew that Phil was now bringing liquor in while everyone looked the other way, including the authorities, since his mother was an influential citizen in their town.

But he feared that the mobsters Phil ran around with would eventually try to take charge of the hotel, the same as the mob had taken charge of many small businesses in Chicago. This thought haunted him daily during his first month living back home in the hotel.

"How deep are you into this bootleggin' operation?" He began the discussion with Phil one day.

"Dat's for me t'know 'n you t'find out college boy, don' be trying' t'run all our lives here. We're gettin' by, okay?"

Johnny ignored the guttural gangster voice. So this was how it was going to be, him and Phil in opposite corners ready to come out fighting, at least as far as the business was concerned. In a way he could see where all their hostility was originating. Maybe he was moving a little too fast trying to manage the place. But he thought he would try to learn as much as he could before he brought his bride there. He wasn't sure whether the surroundings would be conducive to the life they had planned together, especially when he saw Phil dip into the cash register while his Dad said nothing.

"Dad, he's stealing money from the business, your hard work."

Once and for all he knew his pleading fell on deaf ears and decided to take measures to constrict Phil's itchy fingers. He would lock the cash register during busy intervals of the day, especially at lunch and dinner time when the most customers ate their meals. He briefed his Dad on the exact times and hoped he had the courage to stand up to Phil. He then moved the cash into the safe as fast as he could and changed the combination, after he discussed the situation with Lizzie.

"Your brother's goin' to be mad," she said. "Maybe he just needs the change for something like cigarettes."

Johnny couldn't believe how his mother let his sister and brother bamboozle her. He would probably get away with a lot less. God only knew the underhanded, malicious pranks that Aggie was getting away with.

"It must be nice having such a celebrity for a sister, I

can't decide which one's going to be the bride, Agatha or Dell," he'd heard Mary murmur just loud enough for him to hear.

"Shush Mary, keep your comments to yourself," Dell would tell her, always trying to keep the peace.

Johnny didn't like shoveling problems under the carpet. He wanted to know what the obstacles were and get to the bottom of who or what caused them, especially where Dell was concerned. Somewhere along the way she had learned how to squelch cruel reality, and he wanted to know who and when this came about now that they were on the threshold of spending their lives together.

"Okay, John, I'll be ready," Dell responded. She had listened carefully to the tone of his voice for any word that wedding plans were not going well, but she heard none. And even though she was accepted by John's family by now, she was getting more and more frightened about moving into the two dreary rooms at the hotel. She would say nothing about these feelings to John, because she did not want the marriage plans to be upset in any way, especially since their wonderful relationship was at stake. The platonic state they were in at the moment had to progress to a new sexual freedom. The more John would hold and kiss her, the more he would implore her to go further toward the actual act. She hoped when the wedding night arrived, she could dismiss, through their loving contact, some of the barriers she had drawn up against intimacy with men. She was not sure that she felt the same passionate needs that he did during their embraces. Loving him was still basically a cerebral state for her. She feared that he might move toward her against her will out of sexual necessity, and the thought that he would actually enter her inside terrified and brought her at times to the state of revulsion. She also had heard how brutal sexual intercourse could be the first time in a woman's life.

"There's usually blood and you will probably hurt for weeks afterward." Her friend, Sophie, from work portended. "Some men get in there and force themselves, oh yeah, it can be very painful."

She hated these conversations in the ladies's room during lunchtime. They all knew she was about to be married and had very little experience with men.

"Honey, don't worry," another woman put in her two cents. "Your man'll never stray, nope, not as long as he gets what he wants at home."

Dell hated intimacies of her life discussed so openly. Usually she just walked away, but late at night before bedtime, she thought about them.

Was it a fact that men had no control when it came to sex? She hoped that one of these days she and John could breach this subject. Surely he would be very gentle with her inexperience. She and Mary had wondered about their father's aggressive behavior toward their mother. Mom was usually trying to distract him from touching her when they were around. She and Mary often spoke about a couple of their mother's unwanted pregnancies and why women sometimes tried to avoid their husband's sexual demands.

"We don't have that much choice as far as sex is concerned," Mary would say.

"Men are the aggressors and once we're married we have to submit to their wishes whether we like it or not. And I don't think any of these birth control methods are useful. Janet at work said she tried to use that vinegar douche when she first got married, but got pregnant right away anyway. Look at that Martin girl who lives across the street, Dell, she just got married two years ago and she's pregnant again. She used to be so attractive, always pampering herself, polishing her nails, dressed up all the time. Now she's got the baby and pregnant again with that husband to look after. Some of these men are babies, too. They think the women they marry are an extension of their doting mothers."

Mary always thought the worst about everything, Dell thought.

"John and I are different. He's an intelligent man, not one of these coarse immigrants that live around here."

"Maybe so, he sure is different from any other man I've seen here. You may be right. Maybe refinement makes the difference, Dell, we'll see."

She felt satisfied in giving their conversation a positive edge—it wasn't always easy. Defending John's dignity was very important to Dell, however, and their relationship would develop in the years to come. All these people on the outside had to understand that. He really was the first good thing to come into her life. Her job came second, she guessed. One of the things she loved about John was the ease and confidence with which he met and spoke with different varieties of people about various subjects. There were times when she felt about four feet tall as they walked along through Eastburgh, and he struck up conversations.

"Hey Joe, boy, how'd you like the Notre Dame game on Saturday? They murdered Navy. Old Rockne has 'em under control with that offense."

Then he would inquire thoughtfully about a relation he barely knew.

"How is your Uncle Frank getting along? I sure hope he recovers soon, he's such a nice man. He used to wave at me from the porch of his house when I worked for Pop at the garage."

He never faltered in his speech and knew just the right words to say to cheer people up when they were down. As time wore on, Dell realized this was not just an art he had but an ingrained social consciousness to make an acquaintance or touch someone in a verbal way. At times her admiration for him changed to a feeling of inferiority, intellectually, as if she could never measure up to the status he required in a partner. But, regarding human nature or their feelings toward people, they were always in agreement. They had a mutual sympathy for immigrants adjusting to the social mores of the United States. John usually got to know them quite well, helping out sometimes on weekends at a half-way house near the hotel.

"How is that new couple doing, John, have they found work here yet?" Dell inquired. He had told her about their new tenants, Johann Fedor and his wife Nina.

"I think Nina might be able to get a job teaching, she speaks pretty good English. But, I don't know about Johann, he's been drinking a lot lately. He had such a good position with the government in Prague, but he'll never qualify for that one here. I really like these two. I hope they can make a life for themselves. They seem to know so many of the same people that my mother knew, and when she hears how conditions in her little town have worsened, she is filled with disgust for the state allowing it to happen."

"These new immigrants really concern me with their difficulty adjusting. Sometimes they try so hard to make their home here, but if they don't have the endurance to stand up for everything they believe in, it can all collapse. For instance, my friend Stanley Chizmar, I thought he was doing so well, he had almost saved enough money to bring his family over and then something snapped—he started to drink heavily—I couldn't talk any sense into him. I couldn't reach him. I couldn't speak the European culture, even though I knew the language. One of the maids found him dead drunk one morning, literally. This transformation into an entirely new culture takes its toll on the human soul, Dell. Some men have become suicidal and thrown themselves from cliffs behind the mills in Pittsburgh to end all their miseries. Sometimes, it's the humiliation and ethnic slurring names they're called like "pollack, hunky, bohunk, pig-shit Irish." They get no respect from their supervisors at work. Day after day of this life, especially if he's living alone here and is handicapped by the language, to say nothing of the economy, life becomes a desperate situation."

The social structure of the United States was changing very rapidly even within their own town, as second generation Europeans, local councilmen and the police chief became elected and were given city posts. Enterprising Europeans were beginning to gain some social prominence, operating and owning many of the establishments Dell and Johnny frequented, like Kreck's Meat Market and Stalinka's Bakery where they would usually stop for an ice cream cone before walking home. These were competitive and talented people who shared their parent's view of "a success story." They kept alive a spirit of nationalism handed down by parents who had grand illusions of the American dream coming alive in their children, or grandchildren.

Having recently read the best seller, *America Comes of Age,* written by a French Social Scientist Andre Siegfried, John was informed about the progress these people were making. The book talked about America becoming a new world, once again, with the creation on a vast scale of an entirely original social structure which had a superficial resemblance to Europe. It was a brand new age, based on multi-cultural nationalities with religious freedom and even though they were entrapped economically, they clustered together culturally. John and Dell were the first generation who could objectively, at least theoretically, step out of strong European surroundings long enough to look at the good and bad social outpouring in to society and how they would be affected in their lifetime.

That cold January Sunday the pipes froze in the city. Amidst the dark, dismal future he faced at the hotel desk, Johnny walked through the dirty-snowed streets of Eastburgh toward the single warm oasis uptown toward the beautiful angel-woman, Dell. Though his life with her held such promise, his own aspirations were fading fast. He was not sure which way he could turn. Should he assert himself at the hotel at the expense of his family? They were already losing respect for him because of the daily confrontations between him and his Mother. Or should he walk away and try to begin a new career in teaching or counseling? There must be something he could do. Maybe he could reapply at another school for a degree in dental technology. There were lots of new studies coming out of England about secondary infections to the body from decayed teeth. Also, anesthetics were becoming more accessible, so that more people will be going to dentists. He knew many people who suffered with toothaches and crooked teeth because of their fear of dentists. He didn't know if he would go to one bravely. He was not sure if his mother would pay for his education this time around, since it wouldn't be her idea. But she had to have some inclination that his return to the hotel wasn't working out. If he went to get a loan on his own, what would he use for collateral? Dental school would probably start at about a thousand with room and board. He would put some ideas together on paper tomorrow to show his mother. There were a lot of anxieties inside him about how receptive she would be about him picking up and going again and whether or not she would back him financially. It was different when it was her idea. Well, she could only turn him down, then he would probably really hit bottom.

He began to feel a gradual euphoria at what might be his new beginnings. And, for one brief moment, he found a contentment as he and Dell held each other at her front door.

"Get your skates Dell, we're going up to the hollow."

Located in a red clay cliffed area of the Turtle Creek Valley, the water poured off the steep surrounding hills forming a hollow where water and then ice collected. Walking along with only the sound of their crunching feet against the ice, they began the five mile journey. Johnny began to unfold his plan for dental school to Dell.

"I think I can fit my educational background into this profession, Dell. I mean I'll have to take all the required courses, anatomy and all the dental sciences, I'm not sure yet what else. Dentistry is becoming more and more trusted by people and I could concentrate on lessening the fear of people who need work done on their teeth. We could live on campus while I finish school."

"What do you think your mother will say about this?" Dell questioned, watching his face start to redden from the neck up.

"What does she have to do with all this?" It's my decision, I mean our decision, isn't it?"

Dell was sorry for her indiscretion, she knew that Lizzie was becoming a thorn in Johnny's side but did not know how deeply he was affected.

"Alright, you guessed it, Ma is still pulling my strings and I'm tired of it. Every day she's there in plain view reminding me of my failure even though she was the one who pigeon-holed me into the priesthood. I have never felt so trapped in my life. I've got to think of a way to get out of that jail cell, and away from the warden! I have to stand up to her for once in my life."

Approaching the hollow rink, John and Dell could see from a distance a huddle of people, some of whom were pointing to the center of the lake. Johnny ran ahead of Dell to see what was causing the commotion.

"Paulie Woodburn has fallen through the ice," called

one observer. Johnny saw a small head bobbing in the icy water which spurred him into action. Turning around quickly, he grabbed the strongest tree limb within reach. Enlisting another man nearby as support, he held the branch out calling all the while assuringly.

"Grab it, Paulie, hold on to it boy, we'll pull you out."

Dell watched intently with the worried spectators as the small boy held fast to the limb. First one arm then another, sliding his small frame onto the more securely frozen section of pond. Johnny yanked him onto a blanket ready for wrapping, all the while blowing his hot breath on to the little boy's bluish-white face. Rapidly rubbing his skin all over, Johnny felt him fading fast in his arms. Milan Chizmar and Dell's sister Mary helped Johnny move the small body to a horse drawn sleigh. Because of the severity of the winter, sleighs were once again brought out of barns and put to good use as emergency vehicles. Also, many people still did not trust automobile travel on ice.

As the galloping horse threw loose snow up over the sleigh sides, Johnny started to say the prayers for the last rites over the boy.

"Et Nomine Patris, et Filii, et Spiritus Sancti...."

They all bowed their heads in the freezing wind as he made the sign of the cross over the small bundle. Mr. and Mrs. Woodburn had been notified to meet the little group at the hospital, and as the horse was brought to a halt, the hysterical parents ran over to them.

"Where is our boy? Our poor boy," but he was no longer alive to see them. Johnny carried the limp body into the examining room, where he was pronounced dead.

"I'm so sorry for your loss," Johnny said as he walked away.

"You, what do you know, he was not your son," Mrs. Woodburn shouted. "I raised this little baby trying to keep him from all harm, and look, just when my back is turned it happens. He's our only son."

"We tried Mrs. Woodburn, Johnny tried," Dell intervened.

"He used to deliver our paper, what a cheerful little guy, even though he seemed smaller than most boys his age. What the heck was he doing out there in the middle of that lake anyhow, wasn't anybody watching him?" He pulled his hanky out and dabbed it quickly at a tear.

"We're only given one chance, Dell, to raise a child, a little life, and if that life slips through our fingers it's gone forever. That life that we cared so much for, part of us goes with it and if we don't learn to give and receive love, the opportunity goes with the life, it's over."

They held each other sobbing, as they grieved for Paulie and all the sad, lost little boys of the world.

Chapter 8 Celebration

"To the happy couple," heralded Zach, standing and regally lifting and drinking from his glass at the head of the long, decorated table, wetting the edges of his huge handlebar mustache.

"To the happy couple," chanted the family and friends of John Aloyisus Albred and Della Elona Gesner. Johnny and Dell embraced happily and separated, laughingly looking into each other's eyes.

The evening had introduced a well-wishing mixture of family, friends, and passer-by hotel patrons into the cheerful decorous banquet room of the hotel. This special new wing, added on after a prosperous 1925, exhibited Lizzie's accomplishments in the hotel business, elevating her to a more refined element of the business community. Weddings, banquets and other unique occasions, such as monthly meetings of the National Slovak Club, Hibernian Society and executive luncheons for the Knights of Columbus were held here. Walking through the dark hall, and drab functional area used for regular hotel tenants diverged with the striking appearance of a costly Turkish oriental rug imported from the city of Turkestan in Central Asia. It was elaborately designed with pictures of city life in Bokhara and the Samarkand in vivid colors of bright tones of red and green. Deliberately selected for the entrance, the beautiful tightly woven carpet represented abstract scenes of Moslem culture, igniting the curiosity of local gentility such as His Excellency, Bishop O'Hara, who resided over a Knights of Columbus meeting, and the Honorable Mayor of Eastburgh along with other special guests.

Insightful conversations usually began on this spot, since cultivated visitors knew the many skills that went into Oriental rugmaking, handed down from father to son for hundreds of years. Ancient processes were used in shearing, bleaching, picking, and spinning the wool to make yarn, and dyes used were made from leaves, roots, barks and certain insects. Lizzie, who had not outwardly expressed an appreciation for the arts in the past, but she had lately tried to make an occasional weekend visit to Carnegie Museum's art floor. And although it was rumored that steel magnate Andrew Carnegie was a ruthless man to work for at the local Edgar Thompson Works, when he died in 1919, he left his fortune to better local society with libraries and museums. His philanthropic nature interested Lizzie, and his benevolence to cultivate an artistic community motivated her to purchase a religious painting through a representative at the museum. A very tastefully painted Madonna and Child by an unknown fourteenth century Italian artist hung directly across the opposite wall of her old favorite painting acquired for their store in Wilkes-Barre of Molly Pitcher, the heroine of the Battle of Monmouth in the Revolutionary War. The nineteenth century painting by Alonzo Chappell, demonstrated this woman's courage who had taken up her fallen husband's place behind the cannon. This effort on Lizzie's part to cultivate a more refined side of the hard working woman entrepreneur demonstrated itself in these surroundings.

She had taken no chances with this discriminating project, however, this could not be experimental since it involved her business clientele so directly. Consulting with an interior designer from Faller's Furniture store, they had selected some of the culminating effects of this ornate room together: the luxurious long red velvet drapes standing at large windows looking out over the city's industrial sections, pale pink tasseled wallpaper surrounding a high ceiling leading to an enormous concentrically suspended crystal chandelier whose prisms reflected all of it's subjects.

As dinner time approached, the group dwindled down to a singular little throng of two families: the Albreds and the Gesners. From the time they set foot into the vestibule, their commingling was strained.

"How nice to finally meet you all," Lizzie announced, not wanting to ruin all her preparation plans.

Pop was the first to come forth, introducing his wife Theresa who seemed to force a smile. Lizzie walked over and put her arm around Mary, who stood forlornly beside the velvet drapes, leading her to a seat at the long white damask clothed table.

"Now we're all going to get to know each other," came her tactful instructions. She knew only too well the growing volatility of the two families.

However much satisfaction Lizzie drew in expanding her magical world, her pervasive creative instincts still originated in the kitchen where she conducted and orchestrated sumptuous feasts. And on this particular day, dinner was set aside as exceptional, since it was for family. Her majestic culinary genius began with an imported exquisite golden apricot aperitif brought especially to her as a gift from one of the patrons of the hotel. This unique blend had been made near her old village in Europe. The tentative serving staff stood at attention waiting for a flicker in her eye to begin serving the clear consume with delicate egg drops. Congenial conversation flowed between Pop and Lizzie.

"I heard you put this room on back here, Lizzie, but little did you know you would be having this kind of dinner here," he said, pulling a hard roll apart.

"No one knows what the next day may bring," she spoke strainingly, registering her deep disappointment in

Johnny as she unfolded a crisp white linen napkin over her lap.

"Dell's a nice girl, and they seem very happy together." She tried to bring the conversation around in a positive manner. Lizzie then smiled back at Theresa, who sat reticently spooning her soup as though she were just happy to be part of the occasion. Fashionably dressed in a black silk dress, with an intricately embroidered neckline, (which Lizzie presumed she had handmade) her carriage erect looking for something exciting to happen. Lizzie was not sure she had the patience for people who were so silent and could not or would not say what was on their mind. Theresa never uttered a word. What was she thinking? Did she like the food so far? Surely, she couldn't be as angelic as she appeared. What could she possibly have in common with this woman?

"Theresa, I heard you might have made the wedding dress?" This will get her talking, Lizzie thought. She knew she was a little peeved at her and Aggie going out to get the wedding clothes.

"Yes," she said, vaguely.

Did this mean she was happy that we went ahead and bought it? Pondering Theresa's peculiar disposition for a split second, she noticed Phil and his fancy flapper girl friend, Tillie, who Lizzie had protested against attending, had not arrived yet. What could be keeping that boy? Reaching out a bread basket for an attendant to fill, she caught the sullen face of Mary looking disgustedly over at Aggie.

As always, Aggie sat unaffected, her pretty face beamed. She raised her pinkie finger while she speared tiny sausage pieces garnished with dabs of horseradish to her plate. She was in her element, taking part in this royal event, Lizzie thought. Aggie could come to the elaborate occasion looking and acting like a queen. As for Aggie and Mary's encounter that day, Lizzie knew she had forgotten it, since she probably did not connect one detail with the last. She just didn't dwell on any subject very long whether it was good or bad. But, looking at Mary, who lifted her wine glass to her lips, Lizzie thought war between them would be long standing. If only Mary would get to know that underneath it all Aggie was a harmless creature, who had to rely on her good looks to get anywhere. And she did look nice. Even Lizzie had to admit it. She wore a light blue chiffon dress, with fitted long sleeves and a lowered waistline. Lizzie had hit the ceiling when she saw the bill. Mary looked like one of the hired help next to Aggie. She was wearing a coarse muslin dress her mother had probably made. Aggie was listening to Sal, who somehow had managed to sit next to her, much to Lizzie's regret. He was probably filling her head with all kinds of praises, all she needed to become even more vain. She already spent half her days looking at herself in the mirror. Even while Lizzie was talking to her, she watched her reflection. No one should be so in love with themselves, Lizzie thought. She hoped there was a man for her on the next boat coming from Europe, even though she knew it would be difficult to accept some greenhorn for her only daughter. There was a banker, by the name of Samuelson, who liked to stop by for her chicken paprikaś. She would make sure Aggie brought him dinner the next time he came to the restaurant.

Enormous steaming platters of potato pancakes, beef gulyas, stuffed cabbage, and scalloped pork and rice were marched into the room by a procession of waiters holding them shoulder high, then lowering the hot heavy containers swiftly to the table. Oohs and aahs were shouted from all sides of the dining area, which were absorbed by Lizzie as complimentary.

"It's been a long time since I've had gulyas with these egg dumplings," Pop yearned.

"My mother used to make it this way." Putting a serving

spoon back into the bowl of deviled eggs, Lizzie glanced at Theresa, who had finally spoken through some kind of sentimental sigh. Thank our Blessed Savior, Lizzie thought. Her gulyaš had been her best ambassador and she had somehow begun to win Theresa over.

"Have some more," Lizzie said laughingly. "You have to take a big helping to appreciate the flavor, I put lots of paprika in it. What part of the village was your mother from?"

Theresa was beginning to be comfortable at the table, something that Lizzie and Zach always worked hard to achieve with their guests.

"Oh, no. She lived in Budapest," she said. "She was a teacher of mathematics there."

So, Lizzie thought, an intellectual. She thought very hard about what she would say next, since she did not want to ruin the unstable dialogue that had started.

"What year did you come over?" Lizzie continued inquiringly.

"I came in 1900 with my sister, to meet Joseph, he was a single man looking for a wife." Poor thing, Lizzie thought looking into her blue eyes—she came to America to marry. She didn't have a chance to make a life for herself. She had to become a slave for some man immediately.

"How did you and Joseph meet?" Lizzie was not used to calling Pop, Joseph, but she thought she would be polite to Theresa and use the name she called him just this once. She seemed like such a fragile person and not the type of woman that Lizzie usually dealt with.

"Oh, it was all arranged by Mr. Kovacik. We met at his house for dinner. We liked each other instantly."

"That's nice," Lizzie cajoled. I'll bet she never said no to anyone a day in her life, Lizzie thought, trying to think of another subject to bring into the conversation, or someone else to talk with at the other end of the table.

Zach seemed to be having a good time talking to John's Godmother, Susannah, an attractive woman. She and her husband, Nicholas, had been two of the first people they had met when they came here eighteen years ago. They owned and operated Nick's saloon up the street. But their parents also knew each other in Europe.

Lizzie stood silently and began to slowly walk unobtrusively into the kitchen, when she caught the figure of Aggie making a B-line for the door from the corner of her eye. Becoming troubled by her abrupt and noticeable departure, she made a quick mental note to mention this social iniquity to her later. Maybe she had become ill or had to leave for some reason, or worst of all, maybe she and Mary had their war.

All of a sudden gun shots rang out. Two, and then three, and then what seemed like hundreds of thundering bullets invaded their ears. The Gesners huddled together holding each other, trying to keep the fearsome invisible assailant at bay. Lizzie's worst fear was overwhelming her. Could it be those gangsters Phil ran around with, and where was he? He had said he would join them later since he had to see a man about some business. She knew they should have stopped getting that bootleg liquor long ago. It wasn't the Feds that they had to fear like Zach and Phil had said, it was the damn gangsters themselves, and that "good" friend of Phil's, Lonny O'Brien. She looked to Zach imploringly communicating her fears through piercing eyes. Johnny jumped up calmly.

"Now everyone must quietly get under the table, the hotel is being robbed!" Taking him at his word, the small crowd of relatives and friends crouched down on all fours crawling under the table. One more shot rang out. Glasses were heard crashing and breaking to the floor and doors were being abruptly opened and slammed in front of the hotel. Lizzie felt sure that Satan was reigning all the wrath of fire and brimstone down upon her hotel and the city. After what seemed to be a long ten minutes, peace and calm prevailed once again.

Johnny crawled out slowly, moving on his haunches quickly from his corner under the table.

"I'll see if the coast is clear, everybody stay where you are." Fear and foreboding reflected over all the their faces. Theresa sat flat on the floor with Pop's arm around her, she was reminded of a hostile country raiding her homeland years ago. Mary sat in disbelief planning a fast exit as soon as possible from this absurd place. Lizzie, now consumed in a wave of panic, pictured Aggie and Phil and God knew how many others lying dead in pools of blood in the front room near the bar. Oh, why did Aggie have to run out there? Did she answer someone's call? Maybe she heard Phil calling for help while we were all talking in here? What an endless nightmare this was becoming. She looked over and saw Zach speaking calmly.

"Now, don't be upset, we have a lot of people coming through here every day, someone must have gotten upset and may be desperate for some money. Though all they'd have to do is ask us and we'd help them," he lied, knowing all the while it was those damn gangsters looking for Phil. At least for the time being he had quelled some of the anxieties of the people now tiring of their cramped position.

Lizzie took the opportunity to slip out through the kitchen. Creeping through the dark hall, she heard cupboards hastily opening and closing behind the bar. She reached the threshold to see Johnny calling Phil's name in his furious search for his brother. Splinters of jagged wood hung from cupboard doors threateningly, while mountains of broken glass lay in heaps. For some miraculous reason, no one appeared to be injured. Calculating the loss of hotel fixtures, Lizzie estimated the damage to be around five hundred dollars. All this could be replaced and it also might be an opportunity to remodel, blending this area with the design of the new back room. Hearing a whimper from one of the closets, Johnny threw open the shattered wooden door where the sound had come from. A small human ball, revealed squeezed up into the back corner of the bullet ridden liquor cabinet, was his brother. He stooped to the shaking mass, kneeling by his brother Phil, who whimpered uncontrollably. He appeared to have minor injuries, where bullets had grazed his body. Complete and utter terror was on his face. Johnny reached in to his brother with all the compassion he could muster, hugging him with genuine reassurance that he loved him no matter what crazy things he had done in the past.

"They were after you. Why were those guys after you, Phil?" His mother cried excitedly.

"Dat damn wise guy Lon told da big boss Lou, dat I kep da take from da last run up ta da Terrace Speakeasy. He's wrong, I never did, dey dint b'lieve me," he spouted out barely coherent, visibly trembling.

Lizzie gathered her two sons together.

"Listen you two, I don't want anyone to know these things. It's bad for business. People will talk about how those crooks were after you, Phil, let's get our story straight and the same right now. Just say we were robbed and we don't know who did it, it could've been anyone. And it's a good thing we closed the bar tonight, otherwise we would have had dead bodies lying all over." She spoke quickly, greedily stuffing bills and coins from the cash register into a small green money sack.

"Right," Johnny said. "But you have to promise that you're gonna straighten your self out, 'cause next time they won't miss, Phil." John continued to hold on to his petrified brother, emotionally charged with anger for him allowing himself to get into this situation so deeply, but relieved that he had come out unscathed.

As Phil gave his brother his promise to keep his nose clean he thought about the implications of the agreement. It dint mean he'd keep it if some new venture came along, he thought, slowly regaining his confidence. Dem guys just dint know how borin' life could get, but look at him, he escaped gettin' bumped off by probably da best targets in da east, Big Lou's boys. What a death defyin' guy he was. Jest like Scarface, he had nine lives. After making sure Phil was okay, Johnny ran back into the banquet room and Lizzie went to her office to call the police, but only as a formal witness to their "staged robbery." Johnny found their guests had left from the back exit, while Dell helped the waitresses load the dirty dishes onto a service wagon. Lizzie walked in with a pleased expression on her face, as she watched her future daughter-in-law pitching in this way, after all, it was going to be a good part of her life at the hotel. Just then Aggie, made another stunning appearance walking in from another door, as a vision in pink silk, her long auburn curls circling her high round cheek bones.

"Where did you go young lady, that was odd the way you disappeared that way." Lizzie chided.

"From what I hear my timing was perfect getting out of here before all hell broke loose. This place is becoming a battlefield and, frankly, I am extremely embarrassed, besides I had to change my dress. Do you remember the other dress I bought, Ma? That pink silk chemise with the tiny bustle in the back, I wanted everyone to see me in that one, too." She boasted, running both hands down along her skirt, and sashaying conspicuously right and left displaying her new frock.

Lizzie, Johnny and Dell looked at each other amused.

Though nothing derogatory was spoken, the look on their faces conveyed one single thought which concentrated on the self-involved nature of Aggie. The world could be tumbling down, Lizzie thought, and she would have her mirror out watching how she looked while it was happening. Dell, who only looked in the mirror maybe once a day, usually in the morning, thought Aggie was exquisite, but wondered why she spent so much time at it, when there are so many other things in life with which to get involved. But to each his own, Dell thought. She couldn't wait to get to know the real Aggie, there must be a lot more to her than meets the eye.

The next day, Johnny began to rethink his position at the hotel. He felt that his guidance was needed here, especially after the shooting incident. His aspirations about a career in dentistry began to fade as events of a new day unrolled before him. Maybe he could pull the pieces together. Besides, he always felt good about a brand new day holding the promise of a new beginning. He and Phil seemed to have recaptured some of the brotherly love they once shared as youths not long ago. Maybe he even regained some trust from his younger brother, knowing that Phil would never change his ways, but at least they were talking and looking each other in the eye again. He also knew that his mother had liked the calm way he'd handled everything surrounding the "incident," although she would probably take it all for granted and not commend him for it in any verbal way. That's okay he thought, a pleased look from Ma goes a long way for me. I know how this lady thinks. One thing is clear, the future of the hotel can't be trusted in Phil's hands, he'd sell his own grandmother to the crooks for a good price. And I hope Ma and Dad realize it. He has an unpredictable mind, imaginative in the wrong way...always into some crooked scheme like last year while he was away at school, when Phil directed

Honse and Petey Beeler to repaint the cars on the Feds "most wanted" list. He swore he didn't know how he got away with it.

Suddenly he remembered that today was the day he had to pick up the wedding rings at the jewelers. What was he thinking of? In just a few days he would be married. A rush of happiness and excitement filled him inside. Breathing a silent morning prayer, that Dell was in his life providing some stability, thank God, he felt encouraged to quickly run up to the third floor and check out the suite of rooms Ma had designated for their new apartment. They had made an agreement to pay for their soon-to-be new quarters by working at the hotel. He would continue to manage, or whatever he was doing in that dreary office and Dell would help with light housekeeping tasks. Conjuring thoughts of Dell doing drudgery work at the hotel bothered him, but he quickly pushed them to the back of his mind, thinking that it would all be temporary, since business continued to be stable and they probably could afford a new home soon with their private revenue.

The stock market was still soaring and probably would continue to climb, after all the twenties were ending on a note of prosperity with the thirties promising to be even better he surmised, taking the steps upstairs two at a time. But then what if Dell got pregnant immediately? Well there were worse places to bring up children. Was he falling into a pattern of complacency? No, it was this damn good conscience he'd cultivated in prep school. Always questioning people's moral standards, it drove him crazy sometimes. It was hard to have the free will and intellect God promised us all. There was quite a contradiction to theology when it was applied to everyday life situations. He wanted very hard to be the person God meant him to be, but as he took into consideration the opinions of those around him, confusion often set in. Compared with this were amoral people like Aggie and Phil who randomly put their feelings into action, never considering the influence on others lives.

Phil put them all in danger in his association with those gangsters, even though he knew they got their regular deliveries of booze from that connection. But, it was a futile situation. Any one of them could get gunned down out there. Now, his wife would be here and maybe even his children. That scared him. He had to have a private and serious talk with Phil, since he knew his mother wouldn't. She was too busy making money. And even though he knew that she followed her religion closely by never missing morning mass and giving huge amounts of money to the parish, she couldn't see the moral corruption right here under her own roof with her son and daughter. Reaching the landing of the second floor he followed the fresh paint smell to a small suite of rooms. Walking in slowly and glancing from side to side, he thought it was reasonably attractive. We'll be happy here for a while, he thought, throwing himself sideways onto the thin wool mattress, his body vibrating gently with the bouncy springs underneath. Good, no squeaks. He didn't want provocative noises going through the thin walls so that some curious neighbor would be entertained nightly by their intimate moments in bed. In fact, he was starting think about their exposure to every kind of character here, as he and Dell would begin their private and delicate time together as newlyweds.

He pictured them both in the two sparsely furnished rooms. A sofa and a small table in the living room lined one side, with a large, multi-colored round rag rug in the middle of the dark wood floor. The odd looking rug had been crocheted by Dell's mother. It looked out of place there, but they would rather live with it than hurt Theresa and refuse the gift. She had made it from old torn strips of clothing. Aggie had laughed out loud at her gift after Pop had delivered it at the door last week. What an ignorant girl. After all, she was the daughter of a woman who owned this hotel and had once been a peasant girl in Czechoslovakia. Like Theresa Gesner, Lizzie had grown up crafting practical home necessities from scratch. There weren't any fancy department stores in Europe. Furnishings depended on the ingenuity of the people who lived there. If they were getting married there, he supposed he would be cutting down trees to make a table and chairs for their kitchen with Dell weaving materials for bedcovers. As second generation Americans, there were lots of luxuries they probably took for granted here.

There was nothing he could do about Aggie and the way she conducted herself. He often wondered what would happen to her without Ma around? She was only twenty years old, she'll probably meet someone yet who'll marry her, he reflected. And what about his father, what did he really think? Or did he really care? He sat and stared a lot these days, he seemed to be winding down. Would he finally turn out like his father in his old age and just not give a damn about anything?

He remembered when Zach was enthusiastic about the business, carrying out plans about expanding the hotel, maybe even buying that big warehouse across from the Copper Mill on Turtle Ridge. But, somehow his dreams had ended up parked and decaying like their old Maxwell out in the alley, up on blocks never to run again. Wasn't he part of that other era, when drive and enthusiasm ran free? Many people like him had come to America to fulfill their ambitions. To find their "Road of Gold," only to be disillusioned by prejudice and bigotry. He didn't think Zach could ignore the attitudes of some people like Lizzie could. His feelings ran deep. He could be wounded by an arrogant look or comment from some executive from the Plant at the bar.

Yesterday, Mr. Fillmore came in and said to him, "Aren't you a hunkey, Zach?" Now if it was one of our people at the hotel he would have made a comment back, but this guy was a so-called WASP. They were supposed to know better.

"What are you doing rockin' over here, you look like you're miles away? Do you feel alright?" Lizzie asked Zach, feeling his forehead gently for any sign of fever.

She looked into his watery blue eyes yellowed with age, hoping for some glimmer of what was on his mind.

"Ya know, Lizzie, I don't know what happened to us," he said looking far into the corner of the next room. "We used to be honest, good people, now our own son is bringing this reign of terror on us. It's all like a big bomb ready to explode right in the middle of all of us. And we let it happen. In fact, we opened the door and invited the culprits in. We said, please shit on us and rub our noses in it while you're at it!"

He spoke discouragingly, muffling some of the words, so that Lizzie had to listen closely to hear him. It was so unlike Zach to sound defeated, she thought. She put her arm around him, pressing her warm, puffy cheek next to his lean one.

"They're raised here with all this going on, and the bad comes with the good. First of all, we shouldn't have ever let him and that friend of his talk us into getting deliveries of liquor here, and we've got to put a stop to it!"

Zach looked over and his wrinkled flesh turned up around his mouth settling into a smile at Lizzie. She could turn things around. There might be some heads rolling, but she could do what he couldn't, and he was both happy and sad about that feeling about himself. But he was nearing sixty-eight and couldn't stand up to a mouse if he had to. He knew that she'd have to come to their rescue once again.

"Don't worry dear," Lizzie placated. "I'm going to find a way out of this. I'm going to get a load of corn delivered next week and make my own moonshine in the laundry tubs in the basement, we'll call it apple juice."

She had thought about doing that for a long time, but it was just now that everyone felt so threatened by the bootleggers that she would set her plan in motion. Her admittance still did not allay the hurt that seemed to be consuming Zach. Maybe he really was coming down with something, but it appeared to be something to do with his mood. What would she ever do without him as her foundation? He had been by her side practically from the time she and Annie had stepped off the boat. What a monument of a man he had been then. She was the adventuresome one, but he helped her put her plans into action by thinking them through. There just weren't many men like Zach in the world. Thoughtful men who were kind and loving, and listened to people, and really cared what happened to them in life. Maybe that was why they sometimes got trounced on by insensitive people. But that didn't matter, 'cause when they laid down to sleep at night, their consciences were clean. The way God wanted us to be. Even though Zach didn't go to church much anymore, he was a good man through and through.

Chapter 9 Nuptials

"We have a lot of work to do if you're going to wear this tomorrow. Ma, come up and look at this tent on Dell, I can't believe that you let this dress sit in a box in the cupboard all this time," Mary yelled from the corner of the upstairs bedroom.

"Ah, Mary, you're exaggerating, anyone knows that a wedding dress always looks nice, besides the dropped waistline is very stylish this year!" argued Dell, arms held out as if poised to fly from her perch on the dressing table vanity stool encased in the white silk and satin tail wings of the wedding dress ensemble.

Though she felt somewhat luxurious, she realized that her future mother and sister-in-law must have made an error in judgment when they picked out this size sixteen for her delicate slender frame. Putting all anxieties aside she knew that her talented seamstress mother, who had made their dresses since they were babies, could work miracles with this monster of a dress. After all, it was a work of decorative art beautifully trimmed with beaded embroidery and sequined flowers on the bodice, which was a bit baggy, but then she didn't have a bosom anyway. Maybe Mary was right about the dropped waistline though, which hung down way past her hips, but now as she gazed at herself in the full length mirror, she did like the image. This skinny, nothing-to-look-at-girl would blossom into a beautiful bride tomorrow. She and John would become man and wife before God and all of their families. She wondered what he saw in this dismal looking young woman reflected before her, maybe this young moth would mature into a beautiful butterfly while being married to this wonderful man.

"Oh, what kind of a horse do they think you are?" her Mom murmured already in motion pulling the sides of the garment in from the seam with her expert hands, while plunging straight pins into strategic places along the over-expansive waistline.

"Isn't this a beautiful dress. I never thought it would look this pretty on," she glanced dreamily into the mirror once again. "But then I guess every woman looks good in her wedding dress."

Mary stared from the back of the room. "Sure, especially if they've tried it on at the store. They didn't even have the decency to get your measurements or size ahead of time. I just hope this doesn't turn out to be a shotgun wedding in the literal sense, like the other night at the dinner. What a family."

"Now Mary, these people are in the hotel business, they know all kinds of people, good and bad. And robberies occur all the time in this town," defended Dell.

"If it was a robbery," Mary speculated. "Some people think it was that kingpin gangster from Pittsburgh trying to get his take from that hood Phil."

Their mother seemed to be totally engaged in her concentration of how she would restructure Dell's wedding dress for early morning readiness, but occasionally shook her head in disapproval at the conversation taking place. Theresa very rarely had a distinct opinion on any subject, much less the will to interject in what appeared to be a heated discussion between Mary and Dell. Nevertheless, she did worry about her oldest daughter's future at the hotel. She also felt that it would be Dell's duty as John's wife to live under their jurisdiction. Mary could talk all she wanted. Although that was a strange situation the other night during dinner, she thought, John seemed to have the it under control and we did have to trust him.

"Well, thank God my dress almost fits," Mary spoke from over her shoulder. "But then I'm a little bit more filled out than Dell, but I'm not as plump as the darling Aggie."

"She does have a nice figure doesn't she?" Dell lauded.

Mary gaped in disbelief.

"Well as they say, love is blind. I guess my sister is lost to the Albreds once and for all," she shouted, wrapping her thick wool scarf around her neck and pulling her tightly fitted crocheted cloche on her head before stepping out into the cold January winter.

"I'm going next door to ask Helen if I can borrow her shoes for the wedding."

Dell and her mother listened as her footsteps disappeared at the closing of the door latch. They both knew that Mary was the "conscience" of the family. She always struck a chord somewhere, this time it was in Dell. And as she looked into the mirror, Theresa saw Dell's wrinkled forehead reveal a worried look foretelling the life she would live with her contentious in-laws. As Theresa began to unbutton the tiny string buttons down the back of her dress, Dell stepped out to reach for the floor-length filmy veil with its attached satin head piece lying newly pressed across her bed commanding that she pick it up. Standing in white linen cami-knickers and camisole top, Dell placed the fitted satin cap from front to back, and as she threw her arm out the veil fell gracefully over her shoulder and down her back to the floor. It fit perfectly. What a wonder. If the dress was a wrong fit, this head piece had been perfectly made just for her. Glimpsing her from the corner of her eye, Theresa turned to look at her beautiful bride daughter from her sewing machine.

"Look at my lovely daughter. You'll be the most beautiful bride ever, honey," she said thoughtfully, her eyes glistening. Dell put her arms around her loving mother.

"Mom, I'm really going to miss you especially. It's sure going to be lonely without all of you around. I know my life is going to change so much. It already has since I fell in love with Johnny."

They're in love. Good, thought Theresa, because where those two have chosen to live, they're going to need a strong love to get them through. Theresa knew the daily pressures that owning a business could place on a marriage, because of all of those years when Pop had owned a car garage. Sometimes, he never came home until eleven or twelve at night for the long hours devoted to customers and potential customers. Of course, this resulted in him not spending time with the family. Mary and Dell hardly knew their father, not to mention the financial burden on them all. It took people a long time to save for an automobile and most procrastinated in making their decision for a purchase. When Pop first started selling Chryslers, people flocked to buy them but now, ten years later, there are a lot more cars on the market and many more choices to make. All businesses began to be more competitive, especially with all the advertising on the radio. It's beginning to seem that the most business went to the best advertiser and Pop didn't believe in advertising. So much propaganda, he'd say.

Carefully removing the precious veil, Dell thought about some of the traditions she had recently read in a book she had borrowed from the Carnegie Library. The wedding veil was meant to protect the bride against evil spirits with material used long ago to wrap the captive bride-to-be. It told the world that she had been sold and henceforth no man might look upon her but her husband. The veil came to be a disguise the bride could hide behind and, in many parts of the world, ultimately gave rise to the practice of the False Bride. According to this custom, an ugly old woman, her face covered in veils, took the place of the true bride during much of the procession through the village to meet the groom. Today's bride observes a vestige of this tradition by asking her maid of honor to act as her stand-in for at least part of the wedding rehearsal.

Lately Dell had seen many varieties of novelty garters in all shapes, sizes and colors appearing in store windows. Some of her friends would even wear them with their wedding dress now that ankles and calves were being shown openly. The myth perpetuated was that a blue garter, the color of the Blessed Mary, would replace the sash that was previously worn just below the bride's knee to keep away the wandering hands of the groom and his men. Somehow, it always came undone anyway; some scholars theorized that its loosening symbolized the community's sympathetic efforts to ease the bride's pangs in childbirth. Whatever the case, the removal of the sash often led to a melee reminiscent of marriage by capture. Somehow over the centuries the custom survived. Somewhat toned down but still raucous, the wearing and removing of the garter became a high point of many contemporary wedding feasts. Dell couldn't even imagine making such a spectacle of herself, no, she would not be wearing any garter or sash.

She had also read where white wedding gowns were basically a Victorian development. Before that, every color but green was acceptable for a wedding dress. Green denoted jealousy; some argued that green hints at grass stains, and grass stains hinted at an illicit premarital sex romp. In ancient Rome, yellow was the wedding color. During the American Revolution, brides occasionally appeared in red, to signify rebellion; otherwise in the eighteenth century, brides dressed mostly in yellow and blue. In Civil War times, a bride might put on purple, to signify mourning for her father killed in action. A nineteenth-century verse laying out an array of options and their consequences still survived:

Married in white, you have chosen right,
Married in green, ashamed to be seen,
Married in gray, you will go far away,
Married in red, you will wish yourself dead,
Married in blue, love ever true,
Married in yellow, you're ashamed of your fellow,
Married in black, you will wish yourself back,
Married in pink, of you he'll aye think.

With this last reading, she closed the book on some of the silly traditions of the past. But secretly she wished she could have the popular bridal bouquet the book stated every bride carried long ago. Not made of flowers at all, but of garlic, chives, rosemary, bay leaves and other strong herbs thought effective in driving away evil spirits. The bride would take the bouquet to her new home, where she proceeded to set it afire, to fumigate the place against bad influences. Then she tossed the ashes to the winds. What mysticism was this? Dell smiled, wondering what age this actually occurred in, certainly not in 1926 when most everything they planned depended on the decisions of big business. Westinghouse called most of the shots now a days in their town. However, a bit of that magic might just purify their little suite in the hotel for her and Johnny's future. Although for the time being, she couldn't quite name the unseen evil spirits that might lay waiting for them, it was just a feeling and probably didn't mean anything.

Nothing had been traditional or followed the How To Plan Your Wedding, books for their wedding, Mrs. Albred had taken charge on that one. The other reference book she had borrowed was Wedding Plans which had all the guidelines for the "perfect" wedding, starting with the "perfect" engagement party. Ha, someone should have written up the family "cops and robbers" dinner they had at the hotel the other night in this one. And nowhere in the book did it say the intended mother and sister-in-law will purchase all of the bride's ensemble. But Dell understood all of the motives. And the intentions of all parties were perfectly innocent, starting with Lizzie, who was perceptive enough to know that Dell's family just did not have the money to have the big affair that she wanted to have for her son.

The important thing was the beautiful church wedding at nine o'clock mass, with all the flowers adorning the altar, and in front of the Blessed Virgin Mary statue. Then a big luncheon, prepared by her future mother-in-law, and open house at the Albred Hotel for everyone in town to come and go as they pleased wishing congratulations all day. At the evening reception, she was told, there would be musicians and dancing.

However, they would not be going on a honeymoon as the book had related. She could have complained about the omission to Johnny, but thought it might sound ungrateful to him after all his family had done for them. She wondered if the thought had occurred to him. She didn't have a trousseau or fancy clothes to exit the wedding party, as expressed either. She and John would just resume both of their lives together, which she now knew was easier said than done. Dell was not sure how this would happen, but she guessed that they would probably begin their married life in the hotel. Surely it would be easy cooking and cleaning and socializing with the patrons of the hotel. Johnny, Lizzie, and the others all seemed to do it with such ease, but then they were very different than she. Well, they probably wouldn't live there too long, since they would immediately start saving money for a home of their own.

Just then there was a knock at the door.

"I'll get it Mom," Dell called, buttoning her last button and running down the steps.

"Oh, hello Mrs. Albred," she said coming face to face

with the woman who would be her mother-in-law tomorrow.

Theresa reluctantly came down entering the room with her tape measure swinging loosely around her neck, as Lizzie's purposeful voice spoke out.

"Hello, I wanted to stop by to make sure everyone knows what they're were supposed to do tomorrow. What are you wearing, Mrs. Gesner?" she commanded, abruptly, bringing her small frame up erectly.

She reminded Theresa of one of the Czechoslovakian border guards who had demanded to see her passport upon leaving that country. It was now over twenty years ago, but the memory was firmly planted in her brain. Those particular military police were known to be ruthless when it came to keeping order in the country and thought nothing of slapping young men and even women if they were slow about stating their business.

"I made a navy wool suit to wear," she replied with a slight tremble, still seeing the piercing green eyes of the uniformed guard before her somewhere in Lizzie's eyes.

She had even heard stories from her friend Monica before she left home, about how some guards had taken young women into the guard house and had their way with them before they were released. Consequently, when she crossed the border, she'd kept her head down trying to avoid eye contact, but she could feel their eyes on her, shining out at her like the blasting headlights of a truck. And even as she walked through the checkpoint holding on to her aunt's arm, she felt the heat marking their humble figures as they passed through the gate. A faint sound of a laugh hung onto the hollow morning as the guards exchanged words. She could still feel the chill of fear gripping her body, especially when a figure of authority loomed over her.

"Mrs. Gesner, are you all right?" Lizzie inquired,

noticing the sad, faraway look in her eye.

Dell also watched her mother quietly. She had heard stories of past cruelties in Europe, where soldiers had confiscated her mother's family house and land to turn over tothe state. Her mother had been in America for almost twenty years, but always seemed to feel threatened in some way by the freedom of choice allowed in the democratic system. It almost seemed as if she never made an honest decision in all of her life. The state was always there to make them for the people. When she was asked any question, she would become panic stricken as all the options were presented. Dell was not sure how she had come to this conclusion—it must have been in one of the conversations regarding people held in captivity that she and Johnny had had. He had learned in his studies that when a person's mind is confined to controlled basic needs, they don't necessarily exercise any creative thinking, especially if a system does it for them. She thought this was the case with her mother. She arrived in a country with so many choices, to say nothing of the dominance of her husband. She was unable, once again, to make decisions.

"We'll go straight to the hotel from the church," Lizzie continued, ignoring Theresa's sensitivities. "All three priests will officiate, this will be a High Mass, with some of Johnny's professors there, too."

Lizzie's face lit up with the prospect of having all these holy men present for the ceremony, whether it had to do with the wedding or not, it was quite an honor for her, thought Dell. It seemed with her last statement, revealed to them in such a wave of exuberance, Lizzie had said what she really came to say.

We want this all to be orderly, because there will be a team of high class church officials or divine witnesses in the church.

As the hem of Lizzie's black crepe dress disappeared

out the door, Dell looked to her mother for an explanation of her aloofness during their conversation.

"Honey, Mrs. Albred has that arrogant look about her."

"What kind of a look is that Mom?" Dell quizzed.

"You have to realize this, I was raised in the city of Budapest. I was cultivated to be refined, with all the appropriate social skills, which included entertaining the aristocracy. We once entertained the family of the leader of the Hungarian Republic, Lajos Kossuth, who was a professor at the University there and later became the first President. He taught at the University with Uncle Frank and used to come to our home frequently not to mention some of the guest composers and authors such as Franz Liszt, Zoltan Kodaly and Ernst von Dohnanyi who came as very young men, when they were just beginning their careers. All of this refinement was quickly swept away when we met up with the toughened country people hardened by working the land. They brutalized us, intimidating us with their crudeness into feeling we were nothing with all of our breeding. The farmers always felt they were better than the sophisticated city people. They used their might in every way they could against us, especially when we were going through the checkpoints in the countryside. I was never sure how far the humiliation would go. I guess I never felt stronger than they appeared to be and Lizzie comes from that kind of stock. I don't think she's had a weak moment in her life—she always has the answers for every problem in the world. I always had to turn to your father for the answers."

"Yeah, but Mom, you never had a chance. You were married almost from the day you came to this country, Pop always controlled your life, I think he never knew when to stop and let you live life in the American system on your own to acquire some confidence."

"Well, he was here at least ten years before I came, so

he did know other people here and he met so many influential people while selling cars at the garage.
But you know, Dell, we didn't even have a courtship, as they call it here in this country. Mrs. Dombrowski, who was the cleaning woman at our church called Aunt Suzie and told her a nice young man, Joseph Gesner, had been coming to the church socials. Aunt Suzie called him and we met at dinner. The next month we were married, just like that. There was no moonlight and roses, as you hear in the songs about romance. We both did as we were told by our relatives. You kids can't even imagine how different our lives were."

"Did you and Pop fall in love, Mom?"

She always knew that her parents did not have an ideal marriage. Something was missing. She had remembered one day in particular when Pop had pushed her mother rather roughly in front of them. Therefore, she thought she would seize this rare opportunity, when her mother seemed to be opening herself up to her on the eve of her wedding, to find out more about their relationship.

"I think affection to Pop means wanting, you know, to be intimate together," she said sheepishly. "And because of that we don't touch each other as much as we should. We also worry because we don't want to have anymore children."

"But, Mom, I don't see how you can live together and not want to kiss and hug each other everyday. How did you drift apart?"

"Well, I think we probably didn't have the love for each other in the beginning that you and Johnny have. Our first time was not a pleasant experience for me, Dell, I suffered for a few weeks after, and then I was pregnant with you."

"What do you mean, you suffered after that, what did he do to you?" Dell knew she was prying, because her mother began to respond even more nervously, but she just had to know something about her mother and father's life together, since tomorrow night would be her first time with a man. And though she knew him lovingly for three months, this would be different. It would mean exposing their most deepest and intimate body parts to each other. Her knowledge of what actually took place between two people in bed was nonexistent.

"It just has to do with the kind of person you are and whether you were raised in a loving household or not, how can you learn to show affection to your husband or wife if you never learned to outwardly express your love for your mother or brother." Theresa generalized, trying to steer away from that horrible time in her life.

She made a motion to start supper. As she walked away, she had a quick flashback of herself as a frightened young woman ruthlessly thrown down on their brass railed wedding bed. She knew instinctually that this hidden and untried part of her body was not ready to accept the impact of the ferocity thrust upon her at this moment by this man whom she barely knew, much less pit his sexual aggression against her unmatched innocence. Thinking about this occasion years after, she felt that under another circumstance, perhaps with the key ingredient of real love, this act uniting two people into one, might be a beautiful experience. But she would never know. There were examples of men and women in books, movies, and Mr. and Mrs. Orbach in their neighborhood who walked around holding hands and giving each other devoted looks. Therefore, she knew that the right kind of love a man and woman had for each other could lead to loving intimacy. But she could not blame Pop for his lack of romantic qualities either, since he grew up mostly in a callous Hungarian household where ambition to succeed came first, and where a man's aspirations and devotion was found in his life's vocation. Whether it was working the land or with industry machines, hard work was healthy and honorable. Squandering his life away on some romantic notion was reckless. And useless affection was in this category. Procreating, raising a family to generate the family name, was honorable. Romantic ideas were a modern notion perpetuated by the advertising business, Theresa thought, but wouldn't some of these suggestions soften some of life's everyday difficulties along the way?

She'd heard Johnny describe the new Chryslers to Pop just yesterday in his eloquent way. She knew that any motor car couldn't be this great. But if some cold realities could be presented this beautifully, why shouldn't it be? America was a positive country, different from Europe, they wanted to make things right not wrong here. Most American people did not dwell on things that went wrong, but immediately got to work striving to correct their errors, she thought. That was what made it such a progressive nation. The people, at least in her country, were engulfed in traditions and superstitions which had held their progress back personally and nationally. Their attitude seemed so much different there.

She picked up her large wooden spoon, stirring the chunks of floured veal before they started to stick to the bottom of the pan, and poured some warm water simultaneously. She hoped the meat would be tender for the veal paprikaś. I'm thankful I came to this country, my daughters will be able to make more choices in life than I have.

"The Greeks believed that the ruby symbolized the sun. It protects health and wealth and is a high expression of spiritual devotion of lasting love," the salesman articulated, adjusting the ruby ring with his impeccably groomed finger nails, to catch the indirect light of the showroom at just the right angle.

Pop knew it was his sales pitch, but he liked the words just the same. It would be a lovely gift for his oldest daughter's wedding. Some part of them would cross over with her into her new life. It probably was the wrong thing to get her—they should get something for the two of them—but right now he could only think of the loss to their own family. Dell was a delightful young woman, always smiling, an optimistic cheerful woman. She could change his mood just like that, when he'd come in from a low sales day, with a "Hi, Pop, how did it go today? Did anyone interesting come in to the garage or any new deliveries?"

Then he would tell her about some new sports model that had just been unwrapped from Detroit. Dell seemed to be genuinely curious about what he had to say about local potential car buyers, even if she was just being kind to him. He would spill forth all the latest details about imports coming into his garage. The design of automobiles was changing, with more and more of them being made with the top closed, as opposed to all the open air models produced at the beginning of the twenties. It also appeared that General Motors, Ford, and his own make, Chrysler were gradually taking over the manufacture of most of the American cars. Their engines were also quieter and more powerful. Four-wheel brakes, quick-drying paints, sealed-beam headlights, shatterproof glass, factory-installed radios and heaters, independent wheel suspension and low-pressure balloon tires were the latest developments. As he turned in to the street where they lived, he thought most young women wouldn't be the least bit concerned about their father's profession, but he always found himself discussing in detail each new engineered automobile wonder with his daughter. This was why he'd miss her so much, she actually shared his life's work at this point. Usually Theresa was always shut up in her sewing room creating some new outfit for someone, not standing at the door ready to talk to him. He could hear her feet treading away, spinning the humming sound into the household. Her bee-hive of activity occasionally cast its line out into the rest of their lives whenever she missed a stitch or sewed a seam wrong, then she'd yell out, "Ez duhito!," It's a damn nuisance. Which meant whatever she was working on was turning to rubbish. She swore only in Hungarian, that way she could get good and angry honestly, pulling out all the proprietary language stops.

Ah, she's a good woman, Pop thought, but too sensitive for him. She filled all the requirements of a mother, wife and homemaker. What else could a man want? Maybe some passionate sex, which she was never capable of, not even since the first night of their marriage. A very cold woman in that respect, always worried about getting pregnant, never letting him touch her in any way. So what? We already had two children, we could take care of more. I know the doctor said something about her uterus being too thin to carry another child, but that would all take care of itself. And you sure can't believe what these doctors say, either. Medical science isn't the know all, be all that it's cracked up to be either. In Europe they had mid-wives who did most of the work of delivering babies or even a neighbor who was skilled in the birthing process. It was a natural process, the reason why God put women on earth, to have babies and make our homes comfortable. No, he didn't have what it took to be the kind of a guy who hovered over his wife, petting her and getting all mushy with words and outward feelings, what a waste of time. But he worked hard to provide a good home for his family. He walked up the cement walk to the neat two story red brick house. They never wanted for food or clothing either. He had fulfilled his end of the marriage bargain.

"Hi Pop," here was his girl, soon to be a married woman, greeting him at the door. She won't be here anymore, I will be losing my daughter to some stranger out there. Oh, I like Johnny. She loves him, what can I say, except that he better treat her good in spite of that family of his, or he'll have hell to pay. Dell usually preceded him home from her job in the evening, and would talk with him about the days events before she ran upstairs to change her clothes every night. That was when they had their special time together. But this evening would be different. He had a secret, a surprise and he felt an air of mystery about himself.

"Dell, come here," he said motioning her into the quiet dining room, which had places already set for dinner by Theresa. "I want you to wear this on your wedding day,"

Pulling open the red velvet box lid, he revealed the glistening ruby ring, which he thought looked even more magnificent standing on its own, away from all the other precious stones in the jewelry store.

"Here, try it on," his grease garage stained finger nails plucked the ring out of the tiny box cushion and slid it onto her small fragile finger.

Dell was flabbergasted and bewildered by this gift her father had bestowed upon her. Was there some tradition in his country that she was not informed about? Pop's blue eyes beamed with delight at her surprise, as Dell looked into them searching for the person she had known for the last eighteen years of her life. The anxieties surrounding weddings sure brought out another aspect of character, she thought, throwing her arms around his neck in appreciation. He had never been an affectionately expressive man, and after her earlier conversation with her mother, she was overwhelmed with emotion. She tried not to question him, since she knew the loving gesture came from deep inside of him.

"But Pop, you don't have the extra money now for these things." She couldn't hold back the words, knowing their financial circumstances.

"Nonsense, you'll have this forever, and you'll think of us when you wear it," he asserted.

"Dinner will be ready in just a minute," Theresa said, walking quietly into the room while drying her hands on her red flowered apron.

She smiled and looked at the glistening ring on Dell's finger and knew immediately the strength of the ruby ring in Europe. Precious stones were a gift of a lifetime and not to be accepted lightly. They depicted stability in one's personal life, to be passed down from generation to generation.

Chapter 10 The Wedding

Now Everything is you
Everything that touches our lives
Touches us together
Like a violin bow
That begets from two strings, but
one voice.

Rainer Maria Rilke

Twinkling artistic crystal formations resembling large frosted ferns flashed across huge window panes and spotlighted the towering, lavishly decorated wedding cake, as the full winter moon disappeared toward dawn on the felicitous occasion soon to take place in the city of Eastburgh.

One of the coldest Januarys in history would be recorded. Water pipes froze as the townspeople turned in their beds, though their hearts were warm with the anticipation of attending the glorious wedding planned and conducted by one of their famed hostesses. Some said, "wasn't it wonderful the way Lizzie was planning the marriage of the son of whom she had such grand plans," but most who knew them intimately were happy that Johnny and Dell had found each other. They were so alike in many ways: same religion and close in nationality, which was smiled upon favorably by most in the neighborhood. Their courtship had been monitored and approved up to this day by almost everyone and would be witnessed by the same from High Mass to the illustrious reception at the festively decorated hotel. Enormous sprays of white roses, strategically placed, crowded and jutted out from every visible nook and cranny, garnishing the hall and banquet room with a celestial beauty, while linear frames of perfect lilies marked the doorways and windows. An unknown fresh and fragrant haze of sweetness spilled into the usual smoky, sauerkraut rancid air of the hotel. Crisp white table cloths covered the long table holding the celebrated wedding cake, as a tiny porcelain bride and groom stood carefully balanced at the very top sheltered by an arch of delicate paper flowers centered with a tiny bell. The 12" round graduated cake tiers of chocolate and vanilla had been assembled late that evening by an irritable Lizzie, who disdained taking the delicate task upon herself.

The original enthusiasm which had led her to undertake the baking of the wedding cake in the early planning stages of the wedding became dimmed by her actual encounter with tedious handling, preparation of the icing and decorating of the enormous confection. The hours of this singular involvement sent her into frustration.

"What could I possibly be thinking when I took this on myself, when any one of the qualified bakers in town could have done this much better than me," she admitted, whipping the creamy pink icing to spreading consistency while pushing away sweaty wisps of hair with her forearm in one sweep.

She knew that she was ambitious to a fault, an arrogance to think she was the best at this. One of her first revelations was her large, over-worked fingers not nearly nimble enough to move gracefully around the cake's circumference, placing the tiny colored pieces of marzipan constructed into flower petals, doves, and other adornments into the pattern she had designed earlier in the month.

Later though, she stood back surveying her handiwork with a certain amount of pleasure, feeling good that she had overcome some obstacles, mainly the nuisance of herself. This last major task being completed, Lizzie walked over to the big ice box. Inside were stored huge containers of various salads, kettles of stuffed cabbage and peppers, breaded chicken and pork chops ready to cook early in the morning. She smilingly glimpsed the big silver trays of "the hotel version" of savory hors d'oeuvres. They had all pitched in, even Phil had helped to wrap small strips of bacon around tiny sausages, growling all the while. Zach and Johnny had layered the creamy relish cheese spread thickly between large slices of bread and cut small rectangular, round, heart, and square cookie cutter shapes for dainty sandwiches.

All the while as she supervised this operation, Lizzie felt skeptical about how these appetizers would be received by some of the "regulars" who frequented the hotel. She schemed to watch their faces as the delicacies were offered and planned to either ignore them with a mental note about the personality doing the tasting or possibly follow up with a small verbal explanation about how these were being served at the best society weddings in Shadyside and Pittsburgh and don't worry they would get their fill of dumplings and cabbage later. Nonetheless, she wanted to try all the new ideas on this occasion, and it all had to be perfect. She had collected recipes from the newspapers, library, and called some of the best hotels in Pittsburgh to find out what they had served at the last Mellon wedding written up in the Press. She had tried to make her inquiry sound "just between hotel proprietors." Consequently, a special peach punch recommended by The William Penn Hotel, would be served from a colossal crystal punch bowl she had rented from a hotel supply house. This would get them by the Feds regulations on liquor as per her conversation with Sal and add to the decor as well. It just might be spiked with something, she wasn't sure what part of the evening it might take place, probably during the excitement as the bride and groom walked in.

Someone unlikely would slip a little alcohol into the mixture. Maybe she would ask Zach, with his clever soft manner, to do this crafty deed. He usually didn't attract attention to himself and could probably get away with pulling off the stunt.

Lizzie had also heard about champagne fountains being done at very "closed social affairs," expertly concocted to look like an honest-to-goodness flow of water around flowers and statues. But, this would be too expensive and showy for their place and would probably draw some real mockery from the locals. It wasn't as if she cared about the townspeople's opinion, it was just that she didn't want to be seen as "putting on airs" and going too far with the fancy, schmancy stuff and maybe losing their confidence. She might destroy a trust she'd built up over the years supporting the newcomers in their new country, beginning with their stay at the hotel. Lizzie knew how demoralizing it was to be without family and friends you had known the greater portion of your life. But she had grown as a hotelier, too, and wanted to carry out all her ambitious aspirations to keep up with the latest coming out of New York and Chicago. Then there was that political faction of their town she wanted to impress reverberantly, her talent to entertain in a grand way. She wasn't good for merely making big pots of gulyas in her kitchen.

Another concern to her was the growing number of other hotels that had begun to spring up. Even at the end of their very street was the Mazur Hotel. Larger in size, probably close to one hundred rooms and more modern, the Mazur presented a bath with every room, at a higher price. From what she could see, it seemed cold. It didn't offer a home away from home as hers did, or the good wholesome meals she cooked. With her little formal education, she knew all about Adam Smith and free enterprise thriving on competition in America. If you didn't get better, you got beaten. And she would not be beaten, not under any circumstances. "They" could continue to cater to the new entrants to the city, but she would change the cuisine to please a more refined taste. She also wondered what kind of a cook Dell might be.

"Why the heck were they all makin' such a fuss?" Zach had said last night at the bar.

In the 17th century the early Americans in Virginia would just nail a notice to the door announcing they were married. He liked that idea—all this commotion in the hotel was bad for the nerves. He looked over at Lizzie's side of the bed. Huh, just what he thought, she didn't even come to bed last night. Up all night preparin' for the wedding. All these trappings, that was a good word, trappings. It was all a big trap you fall into to impress somebody. Puttin' on airs for the townspeople. He swung the lower half of his big frame over the side of the bed, dangling his warm feet over the freezing January floor. Superstitions around weddings back in Hungary came to mind with all the evil spirits hovering over the bride and groom. The people in his village threw nuts, seed-bearing plants or fruit to get rid of these invisible pests, thinking they'd drive them away. What a crazy damn habit that was. That's as bad as tying old shoes to the back of the car, 'cause the bride's father was mad at the groom for taking his daughter, so he'd throw his shoes at them. Crazy, it was all crazy. Maybe he was just gettin' too old for all this stuff. Was it him? Had he lost his sense of humor? He wondered where and when he lost it. Maybe it was behind the bar somewhere, ha. Nah, he hated it then and he hated it now, he reasoned, feeling old as he staggered to the bathroom. Now him and Lizzie, they had a simple wedding. A priest and two people they never met before as witnesses who had just stopped in for mass that day. No fuss, no bother, no flowers or music, but the main ingredient was there, and is still here lasting forty five years, he reflected. It's not the ceremony that does it, he thought, lathering soft creamy soap carefully around his dark, thick horsebrush of a mustache. Johnny and Dell had genuine love for each other, he could see it in their eyes. He just hoped it would pass the test of time.

Life's disappointments could really sap the hell outta a good alliance. He took his straight razor expertly in hand, turning the blade back and forth briskly over the abrasive leather strop grasped tightly in the other hand, honing the blade until it glimmered to a thin cutting edge.

Johnny was a spoiled kid, mostly his mother's boy, but he was a good man, and he had a good head on his shoulders. He'd told Liz the church wasn't for him, he always liked to have fun and there it wasn't much fun being shut up in some rectory. Those priests always had such sad faces, morbid looking, always in some spiritual trance having a deathly smell around them, kind of a formaldehyde odor, bringing back memories of his old greenhouse days. There was something in the soil that smelled that way, some kind of organic compound. Maybe it was in the fertilizer. Closing in to the mirror, he raised the blade to the soaped areas by the side of his chin and guided its thin sharp edge against the direction of the unruly hairs. A perfectly groomed mustache was his pride and joy. Thoughts of his greenhouse days came back to him, as he inspected his long underwear for spots Lizzie might remark about later. Those gratifying days of potting small sprouts, caressing the leaves of the large ones, spreading love even to the most scraggly geranium in the thick humid room gave him such pleasure. He could forget his troubles instantly upon sinking his hands into the dark, soft fertile soil; the smell and feel of the dark damp texture brought him into union with the earth, his very center. Holding his hand up to the light, he thought he still detected a trace of dirt left under his finger nails. Dropping his long warm woolen underwear shiveringly to the floor, he twisted the brass spigots freeing the flow of water, first the hot then the cold to the right temperature. He hated baths. He only took them when Lizzie insisted. And once a week was enough for him. For one thing, it was too cold these days. That damn Hoagie would have to unfreeze the pipes down there in the basement with that blow torch, start thawin' 'em out at two a.m. Ah, he'd relent a little, it was a big day for all of them.

"Do you want me to scrub your back!" Lizzie called from the bedroom. "Yeah, come on," he grumbled, keeping his voice a little low so those nosy boarders didn't hear him.

But then most of them couldn't understand what the heck they were saying anyway, especially the slang words. Her feet were already in motion, walking down the hall to the bathroom. "

You don't have much time, *dedecek*," she said, picking up the wooden brush, applying it to the glycerin soap and gently scrubbing his long back in a circular fashion. "Ooh that feels good, *babicka*." Her special touch was a balm to soothe his bad humor.

"We're all goin' to have a good time, maybe you can dance with some of the young women."

"I don't remember if I can dance anymore, the old bones are not moving as fast as they used to."

"I remember when we used to dance the czardas at St. Michael's, you were the best dancer there, the lightest on your feet."

"Yeah, Liz, we could do a lot a things in those days. Dancing was just one of them."

It bothered her when he spoke this way and she retorted with some sarcasm.

"What do you think you are getting melancholy about? We have a wedding to go to." And she quickly kissed him on the top of his thinly haired head and was out the door to get dressed or whatever emergency she had to attend to at the moment.

He smiled. She had miraculously turned his grumpy disposition into one of a lamb, as only she could do. Soon he was humming to himself, and looking forward to the day ahead. He loved that woman, he mused, she was the ambitious one, the spark in both their lives. Only one dismal reoccurring thought entered his mind as he stared into the grayish bath water with the scum rising to the sides of the tub. And that fear struck terror in his heart. He would lay awake many a night trying to contain himself from screaming out. He worried that as they were both approached old age, Lizzie might die before him, leaving him to survive here alone. If there is a God, he'd take him first.

Listen to me on this happy day meandering on in morbid thoughts. What was it she said about melancholy? She must've picked that up from Pat O'Connor the other night at the bar. Those Irish were always lookin' for an excuse to cry in their beer. Pat had sung "When Irish Eyes Are Smilin" last week, and yesterday he was bawlin' about his dear old mother back in Dublin.

"Some day they'll make a car tire that will go in the snow and ice," Pop said proudly sitting behind the wheel of his new Chrysler Imperial "80". This beautiful machine had a high compression engine named "Red-Head." The technology was the latest with the engine actually set in rubber mountings to help eliminate vibration. The claims were that it was one of the fastest automobiles made in the U.S. Brand new from Detroit, this one was now veering to the left and then to the right over the icy morning street. The car had been a special order by one of the VP's of Westinghouse and had arrived a day earlier than expected. Consequently, he "borrowed" it for his daughter's wedding. Talk about luck.

He'd let Mr. Goring know in the morning that his fancy new car had arrived safe and sound at his garage.

Phil Albred, the best man, traditionally was supposed to pick up Dell. However, Pop had insisted on bringing his little girl to the church in style, and not with someone who most of their neighbors knew to be pretty near a gangster.

"Look Joe, there's Mr. and Mrs. Rubash and their daughters. They're probably going to the church, they can ride with us," Theresa interrupted his thoughts beside him.

"No, Mom, this is the wedding car, we can't just pick up everybody walking to the wedding."

Mary protested to no avail.

"But we have plenty of room, come on, Joe, stop for them," she insisted.

For some reason she wanted to have her way on this one, Pop thought. And it was a big touring type car with two big seats in the back facing each other.

"Matilda, Paul, you can ride with us. Get in."

Dell squeezed into the corner of the gray mohair seat behind, with her large dress bunched all around her.

"Boy, this is the limit," Mary muttered angrily under her breath. "What has gotten into Ma?" She must feel like one of the Vanderbilts flaunting this car. I've heard people do odd things during weddings, especially when it's their children involved."

Her face started to flush with anger as she made haste to readjust her dress and glimpsed at Dell to get her reaction.

"You look bee oo ti fool," Mrs. Rubash complemented her.

"Thank you," Dell said, smiling back very composed as if they were all going on a picnic together, instead of the beginning of her future.

Mary sat with her arms folded, frowning as she felt Mrs. Rubash's silk laden and lavender-scented flesh next to hers. She used to think her mother had all the refinement in the family, but even she was succumbing to the old country ways.

"What an automobile this is, I'll bet you get ten miles to the gallon with this beauty," admired Mr. Rubash, his red face looking all around the plush interior, pulling and pushing all moveable parts simultaneously.

Millie and Tiny Rubash focused their covetous eyes on Dell, staring intently as if in their own world of dreams. She was a white vision to them, the high point of every young girl's life.

"That's the kind of veil I want to wear," Millie said, reaching over to touch the corner of the filmy material.

"Yeah, me too," echoed the younger sister, Tiny.

Both mother and daughter were named Helen, therefore, the daughter was nicknamed Tiny. And even though she might have been tiny at one time, many meals later, she bore no resemblance to the nickname.

"Maybe you'll let me borrow your dress when I marry," Tiny implored in her babyish voice.

Ha, Mary could not help thinking, little do you know, Tiny, this dress was actually made for your body. Meanwhile, Dell had said of course she could borrow the dress for her wedding.

Johnny looked out from the sacristy, uneven streams of bright sunlight poured through bright colored stained glass windows, each highlighting a dramatic moment in the life of Christ or one of the saints. The largest was Christ's victory over sin and death at his resurrection on Easter Sunday placed over the entry way into the vestibule of the church. Wrapped in a white, loosely flowing shroud and carrying a small flag, his open outstretched arms beckoned all to follow him and live their lives according with his new testament. The church organist began to play a serious rendition of what sounded like Bach to him, when behind him he heard a troubled voice.

"Johnny, Johnny, I forgot da ring," he whispered raspily, nervously tugging at his elbow. "I have t'go back ta' git it."

Johnny nodded his head disappointedly at Phil, wondering how he could mess up the only task he had for that day and then reprimanded himself for giving it to him earlier at the hotel. He should have carried it here to the church himself. His attention was drawn to a spreading black sea of men in about the third or fourth row, their dark suits cast solemnity over the gaiety of noisy, colorfully dressed well-wishers filling the pews behind them. He recognized at least three Benedictines who had taught him at St. Vincent's College and one who he did not recognize at all. He wondered if some were just there out of curiosity, or maybe Ma had insisted they all come down for the wedding. Maybe this would be kind of a lesson to be learned for them. What happens when you fall in love while you're in the seminary? He could still hear the prior saying, "You cannot pull your heart in two directions and still go on one path in life."

The seminarians were all discouraged against having social lives, being reminded that "the more you go among men, the less a man you become." When he'd always felt the opposite, that enrichment of emotional life came from outside their religious community. Also, he'd heard the spirit of the seminary fellowship and emotional nourishment declines in the later years in rectories. It was a solitary life. He often wondered how they could go among people in their parishes if they were not encouraged to learn about social situations. Once again, he decided that that lonely life was not for him—he loved being with all kinds of people. He decided to forgive his mother, too, at that moment. She could never know what was involved in training a priest. There she was sitting in the front row, she and Dad. He wondered how they ever got her to sit down in church, since she had still been running around a minute ago adjusting the huge white lilies adorning the alter.

Just then, at the entrance of the long aisle, Dell and Pop appeared ready to walk down the aisle toward him. He knew it really wasn't her in all that fashionable garb. Dell was a simple woman, and that's why he was standing here waiting for her. But where was his best man with the ring? Phil still hadn't returned. In the meantime, the organist was playing jubilantly, and the priest was smiling at the junction inside the white gate of the sacristy. No one had noticed the apparent disappearance of the best man, probably because all eyes of the congregation were now on Aggie who had begun her slow start up the aisle in a kind of spring fashion show swagger. Exhibiting a kind of reverent strut, she held her bridesmaid bouquet of fern covered pink roses and baby's breath loosely in the crook of her right arm while gesturing with the other arm stiffly against her outline as if held in the motion of a fashionable flounced stanza. Her radiant face expressed her pure delight at being in the center spotlight.

A few of the guests scattered throughout the church smiled knowingly, prompted by the memory of her vainglory reputation, which had resulted in many losses of would-be admirers as they learned that she would require constant attention. The Maid of Honor, Mary, followed Aggie, and joined in the amusement by smiling at the ostentatious style of her predecessor. But hers was a look of vindication, glad that most people knew Aggie for what she represented, an arrogant selfish brat. She looked up to the alter in time to observe Lizzie disturbingly leave her seat, awkwardly climbing over two distant cousins, who'd just renewed their kinship at the warm occasion, seated at the end of the pew. Walking swiftly over to Johnny and then to the priest, Lizzie removed her own wedding ring and motioned Zach to take a place next to Johnny as his "proxy" best man. What was going on here? Mary worried. Then she realized who the missing best man was. What a horse's ass, she thought. This wedding is starting out better than a Marx brothers movie, she mused, watching the moving heads of the people staring every which way apprehensively. She turned her head to look back at Dell and Pop. They still stood giggling together in the vestibule enjoying their moment in time, oblivious to the situation. Should she alarm them, or hope that Phil will appear and everything will turn out alright?

"Pop, you can take your starched collar off right after church. Just get through the mass part," Dell said laughingly, at her father's constrained expression, sliding his fingers around his already reddish irritated neck skin.

"Honey, men were not meant to put their bodies into stiff clothing like this. I'm only doing this for your special day."

"Thanks Pop," she smiled, grabbing the crook of his right arm and walked over to the aisle entrance to the aisle beside the holy water font. She readjusted her voluminous veil around her back, thankful that she didn't have a cumbersome train length wedding dress to look after as well.

"Now what the hell is happening? " Pop yelled, his eyes focused on the newly installed best man standing beside John at the end of the aisle. "Dammit, can't that guy do anything right?" His face was becoming the same crimson color as the inflamed folds of his neck.

"Now, Pop, it looks as if Mrs. Albred has taken care of the situation, let's just walk quietly up the aisle," Dell pleaded, nudging him while trying to soften his temper.

What's all this ceremony for anyway, she thought, all this worry, people trying to be something they're normally not. And even though she began to get glimpses of friends and relations in the pews, she felt confused. It was all a contradiction. Johnny had helped her have insight into this. Why did everything have to be so overdone? Standards of individuals were being lowered for the sake of making money everywhere too. Just last night they'd talked about how good values were changing rapidly. People didn't care who they hurt as long as they made money. This was the web that Phil was caught up in. Fast money. As the thoughts rolled through her mind she realized this was probably the reason she didn't care about the fact that Phil wasn't there. She and John would be married either way and that was the important thing here. Their eyes met, as she, Pop and John all joined hands in front of the sacristy.

"God bless you both," Pop said softly.

Dell slipped her arm through John's, feeling his reassuring warmth through the thick sleeve of his jacket. A wave of what she dreamed of what heaven must be like overcame her, as the thrill of this moment of standing beside the man she loved filled her with pure joy. Oh, thank you, God, for bringing us to your alter, she reflected, contemplating God's design for them, and where each path would lead them. They were on the threshold of a wonderful lifetime adventure.

The cold dark alley stank, as he leaned against the brick wall waiting for Sal. His Best Man's tux was hidden by a black overcoat.

"Ugh, Oh God." Phil squealed, as a rat crossed in front of his shiny black dress shoes. Then he saw him, the invincible trusted man of the people. What a laugh dat was. Sal's heavy overcoat collar was pulled way up. A dark green felt hat covered most of his thin rodent-like face, allowing only the lower part of his eyes and nose visible for contact.

"You got the dough?" he whispered through his rotting teeth.

"Nah, I coun't git it, dat damn Johnny locked de cash register."

"You damn shyster, we delivered the goods, now pay up, ya yellow belly." Just then a load of wash water was thrown out of an upstairs window filled with fish scales and peelings narrowly missing them. Probably crap from dat new Chinese restaurant, Phil assumed. The splash startled them, causing Sal to yank Phil by his lapels and throw him up against the wall.

"Hey, dammit, I'm good fer da money, you know dat." Phil's feet started to sweat in his socks.

"Yeah, I know, buddy, that's why I'm takin' this." Sal muttered, grabbing the tiny velvet ring box from Phil's inside tux pocket and shoving it deep into his overcoat pocket. With that he bounded out of the alley way, straightening his collar and hat as he hurried on to the city sidewalk. Phil stood slump shouldered with a confused worried look, and yet relieved that he was temporarily off the hook. Hmm, he smiled, wishing he'd a tought of dat one. But what would he say to Johnny? He scratched his head. I'm jest gonna have ta lay low, he told himself. Maybe he'd go over and keep Maizie company now that her and Lon were broke up.

The frigid evening brought the excited guests together, as they poured in and out of the hotel banquet room until the early morning hours. In the center, friends and relations stepped lively on the parquet hardwood floor, dancing to the rhythmic Czardas, slide-together-slide, side-step, and the Rida, circling around each other in syncopation with the small tireless musical group. The older couples like Mr. and Mrs. Rubash moved gracefully together remembering with tears in their eyes, an era when mothers, fathers, sisters and brothers celebrated at family gatherings in the old country.

Her face red with orchestrating the vigorous activity around her, Lizzie reminded Zach not to forget to add the "secret ingredient" to the punchbowl.

"Just be discreet, mix it with this, I don't trust some of those new officers on the police force here."

Somewhat exhausted himself from the day's activity, Zach stole away down the steps to the chilly basement. Quickly looking back once more, he reached for another bottle of Lizzie's secret stock of moonshine from behind the furnace and poured the golden liquid into the huge jar of fruit she had given him.

"I'll be happy when tomorrow gets here," he sighed. "I'd like to have the pleasure of an ordinary day in my old chair."

He was tired of listening to all the relatives and town politicians upstairs. Maybe if he was lucky, he wouldn't see most of them until the next funeral or until one of their wives threw them out, and they ended up leaning on the bar secretly drinking their shot and beer, crying their sad story out to him. He could write a thick book about some of their private lives, especially how they weren't gettin' any. He knew who was seein' what woman on the side and where, even that damn suspicious prohibition man, Sal, who was knee deep himself in the bootleg business. So he better not spill the beans on their little penny-anty moonshine down here.

He blamed Sal for giving Phil the idea to get into the bootleg business to begin with. He remembered the day they were sitting around the bar. "We got a stash o' confiscated booze like you've never seen before up at the station," Sal bragged.

"I can't even tell ya how many millions it's worth. It's like money in the bank, a real gold mine."

He'd seen the way Phil's eyes lit up. Bells were going off inside his head and it wasn't long after that he was stayin' out all night on his secret missions.
Now he was in deep—maybe the Feds were even after him.

No one knew yet why he left the wedding so abruptly. He'd seen him pop into the reception a couple of times with some wise guys. What would become of that boy? He might even end up doin' time. And this time, all the clout Lizzie has won't spring him. Poor Philly, he'd just had too much freedom to do what the hell he wanted to do. Zach gazed at the short supply of moonshine left.

"Devil water, that's what you are, and people are gettin' shot everyday for the likes of you."

The band was now playing the new tunes, with the younger generation shimmying and shaking, vibrating across the dance floor to accelerated rhythms of "In the mornin' in the evenin' ain't we got fun," and "Yes Sir! That's my baby." Swinging arms and legs frontward and backward to the Charleston, young couples undulated enthusiastically to the Charleston and the Black Bottom. The older group looked on from the sidelines, some smiling or dismayed by their outlandish behavior. Could they really trust this radical group to carry on their solid traditional values?

"Look at the Rubash girl, she was always so refined," Mrs. Kucik whispered to her husband, shocked at the way the young woman moved to the music. "We could never show up at the communion rail if we had exposed ourselves in public that way."

"Sodom and Gomorra all over again," Mr. Kline mumbled, shaking his head in disappointment, staring intently, thinking, *my life would have been so different if I had grown up with these kids, much more fun.*

"We just never felt free to act openly like this in public when we were growing up," Mrs. Jankovic joined in.

They both turned to look at her, trying to see her point of view.

"I wonder why that's true?" Her husband, who managed the A & P store asked, then he elaborated.

"I think it was because our parents were so backward with their old country ways, not knowing how to act according to the American system. They stayed quiet, 'cause they were embarrassed that they would be laughed at. And they were too, by all the so called real Americans who came over earlier and had to find their way around the social system as well. That's progress for you."

All around the little group nodded their heads listening intently to his insight as he expounded.

"But with this progress goes a faster pace of living, people are spending money like water. They have to have it now, never thinking about the consequences. We're all going to pay some way for all this high living, and it might be a good or bad lesson, depending on how you look at it."

They all stared and believed Mr. Jankovic, knowing he was the voice of experience, since he dealt with all kinds of people every day at his store. But none were aware of the extenuating circumstances unfolding nationally.

Later in the evening Lizzie took Dell's hand and led her to the floor to start the traditional bridal dance. Men and women lined up in anticipation, dollar bills clutched in their hands for a dance with the bride. Dell smiled and laughed as each one danced with her, sharing a mutual remembrance with every familiar person, eventually huddling together crying with Pop, Mom and Mary. After the last dance, Johnny ran over excitedly to the emotionally charged setting filled with yelling and cheering from friends and neighbors sweeping Dell up in his arms.

"Minden j'ot!, j'o uta't kiv'anok!" in Hungarian, "mnoho stesti st'astnou cestu!" in Czechoslovakian and "Good Luck, Have a good trip" in English, crowding around the contented couple all sharing the happiness.

Lizzie was the last to bed in the wee hours of the morning after. Shooing the last wedding guest out, she then checked the pantry supplies which consisted of mountains of uneaten food. Good. She would not have to bake bread that morning or prepare any food for later with all of the left-overs. Locking all the doors and turning off all the lights, she tip-toed up the stairs, following the sound of Zach's clamorous and uneven snores to the bedroom they shared. I know he had a good time, she thought. But as she lay next to his warm body under the feather ticked perinu, a nagging thought kept recurring in the back of her head and now she was finally able to identify it as her precarious balance sheet for that month. For the first time in 10 years the deficits were out numbering the profits for the hotel. She wondered if this was a portent of some new dilemma which would haunt them in this brand new year of 1929.

Alone at last! The wedding had been fun, she had to admit it, even with all the fuss around it. Dell had never seen so many people in one place before in all her life. And now, riding beside her was the person she would share the rest of her life with. They had hardly spoken during the two hour journey eastward, anticipating the consummation which lay at the end of their destination. Dell was not sure exactly what town they were in, just that they had been driving for about two hours eastward, and that it was located near the college Johnny had attended. He had decided that they should spend their first couple of nights alone—away from the hotel.

Johnny, still in his tuxedo with his bow tie undone, whistled a John Philip Sousa marching tune as he parked the car outside the Farmhouse Inn. The weather was below zero, as crowds of dark, tall, pine trees swayed in motion toward the freezing wind and blowing snow.

Checking in at the Inn's small informal desk, they both

smiled at an attractive elderly woman who had been reading and stood up from her chair. She walked over slowly looking suspiciously at them. First at Johnny, then resting on Dell, who began to feel a prickly heat rise from her toes up to the top of her head. Johnny signed the guest registrar.

"And this is my new wife, we were just married in Eastburgh." Dell heard him introducing her.

"Oh, isn't that nice, welcome to Farmhouse Inn, we're happy to have you here. Your room is the second one on the left—The Honeymoon Suite." Her violet eyes were fixed as she spoke almost in sympathy, Dell mused. Can't you look somewhere else, Dell thought, smiling strainingly and wishing she wasn't there. It was as if she had been caught red handed stealing an apple from the grocer's wagon, having to come up with some excuse for being there.

Why did this first time for them have to be publicly announced? And why did Johnny feel so comfortable here? She began to wonder how many other times he had been here and who with, but she quickly dismissed it. Anyway he was her husband now and that was all that mattered.

They walked to the dreaded room where her fate would be sealed, as her first sex act would be performed on the operating bed. Maybe she really was exaggerating, it might be just her imagination getting hold of her. None of the books she had read had prepared her for the apprehensive state she was in. After all, they loved each other, what could happen that was so bad.

The room was bright and pretty. Ruffles trimmed everything, the lamp, curtains, chairs and the bed, perhaps the woman at the desk was responsible for all the frilly trim.

"I guess I'll go and wash my face." Dell said, going into the tiny bathroom with a new brocade valise her friends at work had pitched in for, as her going away gift. She locked the door behind her, and worried about the message this sent

Johnny. But sitting down on the commode, she noticed her hands were trembling, and tried to get hold of herself. Looking at the huge bathtub with an allocated jar of blue perfumed bath salts in the corner, she longed to take a long leisurely soaking. Oh, what heaven it would be to be far away in some other world.

"Hey, come on Dell, I have to go too." Johnny was already yelling from the next room.

"Besides, I want to see what you look like in your new night gown."

How did he know she had a new night gown. Mary must have told him, what a big talker she was, her very own sister revealing these intimate things about her to Johnny. She slipped the black and gold, silk Chinese robe on, holding it close around her. All the while she felt Johnny's piercing eyes staring, making her feel even more self conscious of her shapeless body. She had taken the robe from Mom's cedar chest. Pausing at the side of the bed, she carefully folded the fine silk garment, wondering what faraway oriental country it had traveled from and how Mom had received it.

"Don't worry sweetheart I'm not going to hurt you."

Johnny laughed from the bathroom, while he urinated with the door wide open. Watching him disgustedly, Dell grimaced, making a dash for the white ruffled spread. But before she had a chance to settle herself, he grabbed her in a fit of passion.

"Johnny, I'm scared." She heard herself cry.

"Now, sweetheart, it will be alright, I'll help you through this," he said, caressing her gently in places she never knew she had nerve endings. Loving the gentleness and warmth of his body, she began to submit herself to his touch. This was so wonderful just being close, why did they have to ruin it all with doing the physical stuff. Then he slide down beside her, and began to force himself inside her. Grunting and groaning, he pushed back and forth with such exhilaration, that Dell began to giggle in wonder at his new lovemaking state. Then she was laughing openly. She couldn't help herself, these movements were foreign to her world. This was a side to Johnny she never knew—a man who relished prurient pleasure. Johnny had turned on his back and was studying the ceiling. She was not sure whether he thought it humorous or not. What happens now, Dell mused? Will he try again? Perhaps the morning would bring some consolation. At this, Johnny reached his arm around her.

"I love you, Dell."

"I love you, too Johnny, I'm sorry I let you down."

"Yeah, in more ways than one, " he laughed.

Chapter 11 Beginnings and Endings

"*I*'m happy in my bwue heban," he sang the popular tune of the day, as softly and sweetly as any precocious child given a set of circumstances that might otherwise have altered his behavior. Tommy was a self-assured two-year-old with an obvious sense of humor to match. Imitating some of the celebrated child stars like Jackie Cooper and the Our Gang comics now gracing the big movie screens, he would dress up in any one of the extra large coats and hats hanging on a rack nearby, and with only the lower half of his baby face showing, would walk by the afternoon lunch customers. His antics brought a giggle from all corners of the room. Laughter was a rare commodity in the dark days of the Depression. The hotel patrons roared and clapped at his high jinx, sometimes giving him a penny. These spectacles made Dell furious. One day right in the middle of his two penny opera, Tommy peed in Mr. Greenwald's new white Stetson hat. Everyone laughed uproariously, except Mr. Greenwald, who walked over to the soaking hat, emptied it into a nearby brass spittoon, and put it on his head, shouting all the while as he walked out.

"Lizzie, you're gonna pay for the cleaning and blocking of this hat."

"Sure, Henry," she replied, stifling her own chuckles and patting Tommy on the top of his fine haired brown head. "Send us the bill."

But one quiet observer, even though she smiled in pretense, did not think it quite so funny as she walked over and scooped up her young son, taking him upstairs. Dell was filled with mixed emotions: mostly unhappiness over the child being exposed to the kinds of unsavory characters found around the bar. She had just gotten used to calling this place "home," however, the daily onslaughts of Lizzie would prevent that from ever happening.

It's no place to raise a family, I'm going to have to lock Tommy in the room upstairs again. A young child shouldn't be among the drinking and smoking men at the bar, with every other word a swear word, she told herself resentfully.

Dell had discussed the situation with Johnny more than a couple of times. Johnny would just shake his head.

"You know our plans for moving to our own place fell through with the Market crash, Dell. As soon as things get a little better, we can start to think about buying a place of our own."

His brown eyes twinkled. But he knew it would take a long time for anything to get better. He was frustrated that she didn't understand. The country was in the middle of a serious Depression. They had all just listened together to the radio in the kitchen. Another stock market executive killed himself. This one took place in the Union Trust building in Pittsburgh where many brokerage offices were located. The building was patterned architecturally after the cylindrical design of a Belgian cathedral: twelve floors high, with a large light well extending down the middle from skylight to lobby. On each floor, the board rooms of the brokerage offices were like auditoriums, with long and wide open exits going out toward the light well, which was bordered by a waist-high railing.

The news report said, "Yesterday, Homer Rossiter, fifty-six, a stock speculator with Moore, Leonard and Lynch, after seeing his investments dissolve before his eyes, fled the boardroom and went over the railing to his death."

This kind of headline glutted the newspapers day

after day. And even in their own town, they had just last week witnessed the suicide of Phil's friend, Lonnie O'Neil, who had jumped 200 ft. to his death from the nearby, huge concrete arched Westinghouse Bridge, which spanned across the valley. At least they thought it was suicide, no one had actually seen it happen.

"He owed 'em da store." Phil spoke, shaking his dark, oily head slowly, suddenly realizing the poor sap could have been him.

"Poor Lon, he was too kind and tame fer 'his own good. He put his last "take" 'all in da market. He lost it all, even de ten tousand he owed de mob."

Johnny and Lizzie sat together pouring over the diminishing profits of the hotel books. He had never seen his mother so compliant.

"I had to reduce the rooms again last week. The men out of work cannot pay. Thank God I kept my money out of those banks. Look how they all closed down, and with all the poor people's money still in them? Everyone laughs at some of my old country ways, but this time I can laugh."

Lizzie pursed her lips with every tiny wrinkle around her mouth standing at attention and shook her head knowingly. Johnny had to acknowledge her perception as well, as slanted as it was.

"My cash will last for a few years, I hope, until things get better, since we'll have no new profits coming in for a while. Our regular customers will probably go to live with relatives or friends. People are doubling up in their homes, just to get by. And some of the nicest families in town are waiting in the soup line at the kitchen back door. They are not just vagrants any more."

"I know, Ma, the last count was almost 12,000,000 people out of work and almost 32,000 businesses bankrupt.

Westinghouse stock sank from 289 in September to 102 and U.S. Steel from 261 to 150, last count."

Leave it to Johnny to know the numbers, Lizzie thought.

"Okay, John, but we can't sit and talk about it all morning. Let's see what else we can cut out here in our deficits."

He now looked at her stern face and was reminded of a personal matter that needed to be settled.

"Ma, I wish you'd take it easy on Dell. She's on her feet from morning to night in that kitchen."

She stared back at him, now her old superior self.

"**You** take it easy on her," she said. "She's pregnant already again, second time in over a year."

His face reddened. She was heartless. Leave it to her to fling it back in your face.

"Ma, I'm sure Father Flanigan approves of the way we're living."

"Alright, then don't be blaming me for tiring out your little wife," she said, moving her short stubby fingers along the long accounting ledger, indicating to him to get down to business.

At that moment one of the maids stuck their head in the office door.

"Mrs. Albred, there's a delivery truck in the back alley with a big order of potatoes. The driver says he's afraid the people back there will grab the sacks as he unloads them."

"Okay Millie, I'll show him where the chute is and make the poor boy feel secure. Thanks. Johnny, keep at it here."

She stood up slowly from her chair. Ma's getting old, he thought, she doesn't have the vitality she once had. But she'll still never compromise on anything. And I know she's still harboring resentment about me not being a priest, that's why she treats Dell like she does. But he couldn't worry about her reprisals anymore. His life had changed, he now had his own family. It was different. He had to be responsible. John knew Dell was taking the brunt of things around there. Just the other day she'd cried about Aggie leaving in the middle of evening meal preparation.

"Some red-headed man came over to the kitchen door, just stuck his head in and called her," Dell said. "I guess she went for a walk or something with him. Anyway, Lizzie had asked her to get all these vegetables ready, which included peeling ten pounds of potatoes. When Lizzie came in about an hour later and saw the pile still there, she just yelled out, she was really upset. I was trimming some apple pies. She knew I had been busy, but she blamed me because I was there looking at what Aggie hadn't done. She never said a word to Aggie about it when she came in later. How can she be that way?"

Johnny knew how wicked his sister could be. She had managed to learn every trick to get around their Mother's domineering ways, so there was no use talking to her. She seemed to be so devious. She never gave a damn about how she treated other people. It was hopeless, but he had no idea how to solve it. He hated being complacent, consequently, indifference had become his status during the last year. For one thing, he found it belittling to have to take orders from his mother everyday, and also to work ten hours a day at a job that was not of his choosing. The fact of the matter was that there had always been plenty of money available in his life. He never had to worry about where his next dollar would come from, like now. All their hopes and dreams for a house had been dashed by the Depression. They were lucky to have a roof over their heads and three square meals. When would it all end?

Their life together had started out almost perfect after their wedding. He remembered their first night together navigating over the freezing, icy roads to the little Village of Ligonier near his old campus of St. Vincent. It was about a 50 mile drive, so he had made the reservation early, knowing the weather might be a cruel factor. He'd always wanted to come to this Inn, but it had to be with the woman he loved. The scene had been set, a sizzling, scintillating fire, a late night snack and champagne to relax them both. If only his own selfish ego hadn't gotten in the way. He could feel Dell tense up as they entered their room. She vanished into the bathroom, for what seemed like an interminable amount of time. He'd finally had to coax her out. And when she did emerge, she was all wrapped in a black and gold, silk Chinese kimono which clung to her sensuous looking body. He felt completely aroused just casually glancing at her walk across to the bed. He had held himself in control for so long during their short relationship, wanting to go all the way every time she was near, that his brain knew it was time for sweet relief.

Eventually, she removed the kimono, but only after she was safely under the covers. Conscious that his presence disturbed her, he popped the cork on the champagne, spilling out two glasses of the sparkling liquid. Taking two large steps back to the bed he stumbled on the rug, falling across the bed showering himself and Dell as well.

"Oh, no. Johnny, are you alright?" Dell sat up laughing, expensive liquid dripping down her hair and chin. Johnny caught sight of his bride in her weakened state and lunged over, kissing the streaming liquid away from her neck and shoulders. She now wore a streaky, wet and clingy pink satin nightgown with a lacy rose wilting below the neckline. Seizing the spontaneity of the moment, he anxiously assumed his position along side her.

"You look nice." He crooned softly, putting his arm around her.

"Thank you." she murmured, shyly folding her arms

in front of the revealing material. Shimmering, reflective flames from the fire shot up the walls, as they snuggled up under the heavy quilt. Johnny was surprised at his own nervousness. Here it was his night of nights, and he was actually orchestrating the next move with the woman he loved. *Maybe I should have carried her over to the bed like Douglas Fairbanks,* when we first entered the room, he thought. Still worrying about her reaction, he remarked clumsily,

"Let me know if I do something you don't like."

"Okay," she said. Then he continued to caress her, she responded as if she liked it. Positioning his body next to hers, he thought she was ready, but found she was as tight as he might have been after five beers. Then she became hysterical—or was she really amused at his efforts? Why couldn't she understand how badly he wanted her? He had truly wanted to make her happy during their lovemaking, exciting her senses to the point of no return, experiencing the ideal sexual experience as they climaxed together.

It wasn't until a month later that they finally consummated their marriage. He had to take into consideration that everything connected with sexual stimulation to her was completely new. He had to take his time approaching her romantic feelings. Even to this day he felt that she had just been going through the motions to please him. He wondered if she even knew how to anticipate a climax in their lovemaking? He had wanted their sex life to be wonderful, and it was, at least for him. But now here she was expecting their second child already and probably starting to view their intimacy as some kind of threat to becoming pregnant every time he came near her. Their life together was not as romantic as when they started out. Most of the time they were both too tired when he climbed up the steps to their little rooms after working in the hotel all day. Nevertheless when he put his arms around her, especially now with her thickening waistline, he knew that he loved her and their son more than anything else in the world.

A shrill telephone ring alarmed him out of his thinking.

"Hello, he said. "Oh, hello, Pop, yeah, come on down this afternoon, we can talk then."

This was unusual, Johnny thought, Pop Gesner never actually called a meeting for their casual conversations. But that afternoon, Pop insisted on a quiet place for them to talk.

"Dell looks awful, Johnny, what the hell are you guys doin' to her down here, using her as a servant? I don't like it and we're thinkin' of bringing her back home again until you get a place for your family. And frankly, I think you should go out and get a decent, honest job."

Looking into Johnny's downcast eyes and the wrinkled frown spreading across his bushy auburn brows, he knew he had struck a chord with the young man. Pop knew he could be honest with him. After all, Johnny'd worked for him long enough to know he would want to do the right thing by his new family.

"Now I know what you're gonna say about the Depression and all, but there are some jobs at Westinghouse. I happen to know the management is looking for a security guard over there at the MX-15 gate. My friend Jack O'Connor, was just in the garage the other day trying to buy a used Chrysler. Huh, I remember when he bought a new one every year. This damn Depression. Well, anyway, he'll talk to ya about the job. Whatdaya think?"

"I wonder if it will be okay with Ma if I only work days or something like that?" John said, stalling for time, feeling the floor falling out from underneath his firmly planted feet.

"Ma? Ma?" Pop said incredulously, now sitting halfway

off his chair with his reddening face hanging out disproportionately toward Johnny.

"Johnny, your family is going to leave you." He didn't really think that Dell would leave Johnny, he hadn't even asked her, but continued.

"You have to leave this place and start looking out for your own. It's time to grow up, my boy."

He then stood up not knowing the real consequences of his message. He hoped it would fall upon fertile ground. Johnny numbingly felt lights flashing all around him. Pop's heavy hand patted him on the back and he heard him go through the door, probably to the bar for a "stiff" one.

It was Friday, Helen's day off. Dell hated this day since she would have to fill her place waitressing in the front dining room. Johnny had already gone downstairs to help Zach tend bar and Tommy lay in his crib almost asleep. She began to dress, throwing the ugly black size fourteen over her head, pulling it down around her large middle. She wondered why there weren't more nice clothes made for pregnant women. After all, many women spent a good part of their lives pregnant, why couldn't someone pay attention to their poor big bodies. Her belly was obvious and awkward-looking because the rest of her body was so thin. Feeling sad at her uncomfortable and handicapped state, she stood sideways in the large vanity mirror. Her image looked as if there was an adjoining hillside growing out from under her now embellished bosom.

I feel so miserable I wish I could stay up here and sleep all day, playing with Tommy or baking cookies and doing what a real mother might do.

She didn't want to be with all of them down there. Morning sunshine was streaming in through the window—maybe she could even have taken Tommy for a walk today.

She and Johnny had fixed their little rooms up cute, she smiled, looking around the kitchenette with its plaid curtains and matching tablecloth her mother had made. And for the most part, she was pleased with their life together. If only they could be alone. They also had bought a three piece oak bedroom set, with a vanity dressing table and blue silk brocade upholstered stool where she could sit to comb her hair with a white onyx brush, comb and mirror that Pop had given to her on her fourteenth birthday. Pop had loved to buy gifts for Mary and her. A tear came to her eye when she thought of her father and mother at home. She missed them so much. She knew that John didn't understand how many adjustments she made to live there with his family, working hard day after day in the hotel. She loved him more than ever, but he had never left his home, he'd just moved his clothes upstairs. She prayed every night that she would fit in with them, but there seemed to be so much contention amongst them all, much less acceptance of her into the family. Especially, from his mother. She seemed to find fault with everything she did, nothing was ever clean enough. She could never satisfy her demands. Lizzie appeared to walk around like some sort of machine, insensitive to everyone around her unless they held some usefulness for her hotel's needs. She had appealed to her mother-in-law in a quiet pleading voice.

"Ma, I really don't want to walk in front of the men in the dining room looking this way I'm getting too big and some of them just leer at me across the bar. I'm too embarrassed."

But Lizzie showed no concern. With her hair wrapped up in a white babushka, a few strands of dark hair escaped from a side fold. Though she was now over sixty years old, she was still a vibrant woman. Dell noticed the large distorted bone extending out of her right wrist, probably from years of the pressure of grasping the side handles of her rolling pin.

Lizzie pushed small, buttered mounds of dough, flattening them to a smooth level for cutting into proportionate squares. Working at great speed, she didn't even look up into Dell's eyes, as a touch of flour crossed her nose. Dell had recently begun to fear her proximity, a sudden footstep on the linoleum made her shudder. She worried daily about such an encounter occurring when she was not working at great speed, which was now often since she was very tired most of the time.

She and Johnny had been so wrapped up in each other their first year married and then they'd had Tommy in November the same year. It seemed she'd had a couple of bad cramps and there he was. But this second time, she was nauseous for the first three months, had gained a lot more weight and was more sensitive to everyone and everything around her. She just didn't feel like the same person who had come here to live last year. Even though she saw Aggie sneer at her on that first day and look toward her mother in distaste, she'd tried to forget that moment.

"Oh well, " she braced herself, *"guess I'll go down and tend to the lunch time crowd."* She waddled down the steps like a big mother duckling with her wings out, stomach thrust forward making her way down the old wooden steps. But as she placed her low-heeled oxford on the last step, an excruciating pain shot up her back suspending her in its clutches. *The baby must be coming,* she thought as pain seized her body. "Ohhh, ooo," her cry rang out in the dark hallway.

Crumbling on to her haunches on the first step not wanting to draw attention to herself, she felt the vibrations of moving feet very close over the hardwood floors. It was eleven-thirty, everyone was busily preparing for the factory people who would come through the door in hoards. Lizzie would wonder why she hadn't shown up on time for work. She would probably throw a fit and come looking for her.

Johnny was probably helping Pa tend bar. If only she could signal to someone to bring him to her, but no, this was the busiest time of the day, and no one could see her there with her knees pulled up on the other side of the large dark wood banister.

She awoke to excruciating pain as her body arched convulsively with her agonizing.

"Now, Dell, push down," she recognized Dr. Brown's voice.

She pulled tightly on the sheets around her, ripping them, shredding them in strips.

"Ahhhh," a final cry released her, she felt her body throbbing as it separated itself from the source of the suffering.

"Dell, we have another boy, a perfect big boy," Johnny whispered lovingly into her tear streamed hair matted face.

Drifting into soothing blackness, she was pleased with herself, knowing the supreme important purpose of being a woman.

Baby Benedict was a big bundle of joy. He seemed to know the pain his mother suffered in his delivery, hence he would remain a contented little boy who slept and ate at all the right times. He was loved not only by his parents, but especially by his Grandpa Zach, who would sneak into their bedroom after Johnny went to work, pick him up and rock him for long periods of time. Dell would spy him creeping past her bed while she had her lying-in. They had a rapport that Dell watched quietly with astonishment. He would talk to the tiny baby, singing and laughing and finally a tiny red hand would reach up to grasp his great waxed mustache. As Dell watched him, Zach turned into a magical person, not the constant purveyor of favors and deeds at Lizzie's request that she thought him mostly to have become. She knew he and Lizzie were devoted to each other, but when she was on the rampage everyone suffered, even Zach. He was a gentle, loving human being. It was during this time that he and Dell began to get to know each other, aside from the demands of the hotel.

"Why don't you two ever take a break away from here? We can manage the place." She would usually begin, since he was content never to say anything for long intervals at a time.

"Dell, you have to understand, even if our country was not going through the depression, we come from the bourgeois, the middle class. We are the people who make the world go round. We work so that all the others may live their lives comfortably. And Lizzie, well, Lizzie works because she thinks no one else can do it as well as her, and it's true. Who else has the strength?"

"But if the work and drudgery is getting her down so that she is starting to yell at other people, including myself, is that something she should continue to do?"

Zach put his head down, and Dell realized she had gone too far. She had breached his ethics. He would never talk against Lizzie in any way. Just then, they both laughed as the miniature Charlie Chaplin, Tommy, walked in with Johnny's sharkskin suit coat dragging on the sides and his big black dress shoes clomping as he tried to walk across the room.

"Do you think Tommy will become a star on the Broadway stage or in the movies, Zach?" his laugh ended teary-eyed.

"Neither. I think he will own his own nightclub. See how much joy you and Johnny have brought us?"

"What joy? What do you think you're doing hiding up here?"

Lizzie put her head in the door ready to bawl them

both out, when Tommy saw her and dragged his oversized feet across the room.

"Baba, you have candy in your apron pocket for me?"

He was swept instantly up out of his enormous shoes into her arms and covered with kisses and hugs as she rocked him spontaneously all the while.

"Det atko. Oh no, sweet boy." She unwrapped a red lollipop. Then, as quickly as she had picked him up she put him back into his big shoes once again and held her arms out to Zach.

"You are always getting away to come up here, "Mr. Sneak away, now it's my turn to hold this little bundle. Look at him, hello," she cooed. "What a rascal, he's going to be a bad one, I can tell."

Benedict's little brown eyes watched her every move, and he even managed a crooked smile as saliva mixed with milk dribbled out of his tiny mouth.

"Isn't he a happy boy, he's going to be fun, oh boy, is he going to be fun." Her voice changed into high and low tones.

Watching this sight between Lizzie and Benedict, with Zach's lips shaping the same word sounds Lizzie spoke, Dell lay on the bed looking on in wonder that this could be the same woman who scolded her daily, like the way Lizzie'd carried on last week when she hadn't hung the pots and cookware up with their handles pointing in the same direction. Dell thought she had an obsession about some things, but when she'd mentioned this to Johnny, he'd been defensive.

"Oh, we all know how Ma is, she's always been very thorough in her work, making sure every utensil is shining afterward. It's not you Dell, It's just the way she is."

Once again, she listened as he rationalized his mother's behavior.

"Oh, by the way, Dell, we may need you to do your

sewing later this afternoon. Do you think you can make it downstairs to the sewing machine?" Lizzie interjected.

Dell shook her head slowly, half-smiling and acknowledging her part in their scheme to hide their supply of moonshine under the trapdoor in the hall. Their old prohibition officer, Sal, who had been their informant, had recently been found guilty of selling bootleg liquor. A new man was assigned to their district and they weren't taking any chances. Dell was always assigned as a decoy sitting on a braid rug over the suspicious trapdoor. She presented the image of the dedicated seamstress, while the man inspected the premises for the home-brewed hooch. In the meantime, Zach and Johnny had turned the huge bar around, making all premises look free of suspicion.

Sal wasn't alone, the Treasury had just announced it had fired 706 agents and would prosecute another 257 for taking bribes from speakeasy owners. But it was a loosing fight; they all knew Amendment 21 would be passed by the end of the year, turning the problem of controlling liquor traffic back to the states. Meanwhile, Phil's hero, Al Capone, was counting his profits and valuables with his 11-1/2 carat diamond ring and steel plated custom-built $30,000 limousine at his mansion in Chicago's Grand Crossing District. His gang had "rubbed out" all possible competition on February 14th, the St. Valentine's Day Massacre, when Capone's hit men gunned down seven members of the rival Bugs Moran gang in a classic underworld execution. Phil had stayed close by the radio listening for details of his hero's escapades.

Good thing I've kept my nose clean, he thought. I knew Sal'd get pinched. He was a pushover for that undercover Fed. I could tell he was all wet the first time I saw 'im.

He'dfinally got Dell's ring back—after he found a load of money in Ma and Pa's mattress to trade for it. Oh well, it was all water under de bridge now. He'd given it back to da happy couple a few days afta the weddin'.

Whew dat was a close call, I Had da heebie-jeebies for a few days when I told 'em all I lost it, and was late for da wedding 'cause I was takin' da car seat out lookin' for it. I thought Ma'd get hep to da story, she must be gettin' ta be a flat tire believe'n all that applesauce. Boy, I'd sure like ta woik fer Capone, he's a hard boiled guy, but he's makin' his fortune fast. After Ma and Pa kick the bucket I could run the joint as one of Capone's point of interests.

Once again tonight Lizzie had been wakened out of a deep dreaming sleep. She had been gathering fresh vegetables from a garden outside her home in Ryka for a special dinner. She looked out into a magnificent lush jungle of vegetables. There within her reach were rich luscious ripe red tomatoes, peppers, radishes, and beets growing to gigantic proportions. Peas and beans crawled high to the sky on enormous telephone poles. And the corn looked like huge swaying palm trees, tassels blowing wildly. Leafy green lettuce lavished every corner of the garden, waving their large leaves for her to come to pick them. Cucumbers, melons and squash piled high in another corner. All had faces with large mouths shouting, "Pick us, we're best, forget the rest."

Suddenly, an altercation broke out between the green and red vegetables, a butchering took place. Tomatoes squirting like blinding rain flowed across the field, peas pelleted and asparagus spears pierced soft beets which bled openly. Celery soldiers stalked into the quagmire, trying to bring order to the chaos—sloshing and chopping, scooping and slushing through the massacre. In one split second between dream and reality, she realized the coughing and choking was next to her, as torrents of chilling autumn rain hit the window in blinding sheets.

"Oh, you sound worse tonight," she said as she

stretched a pink flannelette arm out from under the covers.

Feeling his forehead sympathetically, she was gripped by fear as she felt the heat on his temple. Then seeing his brownish-red stained handkerchief lying next to him her panic was confirmed.

"How long have you been spitting up blood?"

"Ah, just...the last...couple of days, " he answered, struggling to get out each word as he breathed raspily between each one. He stretched his long arm up, covering his red, watery eyes and forehead.

"I'm okay, Liz, its this damn coal dust still in my lungs, or whatever it is from the mines. It'll go away, it always does."

"I think this is the day you stay in bed," Lizzie commanded."

"Aye, aye, Captain," Zach sputtered out between coughs, pulling the fluffy white perinu up close under his chin and over his yellowish stained long johns. An arrow shot through her heart looking at her big staunch husband knocked out by this illness. She knew he had bouts with asthma especially now in the Fall, but always seemed to conquer them with a day in a warm bed and bowls of her hot chicken soup. But this time she was worried, calling Doctor Stein before she put the plump chicken in the kettle for soup. As if Stein could perform some miracle, she trusted his quackery about as far as she could throw him. But this time she'd call in the militia if she thought they'd be able to cure her husband. She began to panic inside. *Now get hold of yourself, he's still a healthy man—he's lived all this time with this ailment—I know how to get him through another crisis.*

"He's in the early stages of pneumonia, Elizabeth."

Lizzie blinked, knowing she could have diagnosed it.

"You can tend to him in his illness, but pneumococcus can be contagious and chances are you have already been exposed to more than your share. I advise you to sleep in another room at night."

Lizzie immediately felt sorry she had called him. All these doctors did was read the Doomsday Directory and scare the bejesus out of us.

"Doctor, I've lived with this man for a long time now. He had this `black lung' when I met him. I'm used to him coughing at night, its just the cooler weather coming in—he'll get better as soon as the seasons change. By December he'll be his old self again. We know what to do for him here, thank you for your time."

Why had she been so impulsive and run to the telephone? Dr. Stein glared at her suspiciously down his long nose and through the bottom of his pince-nez.

"Elizabeth, you are a stubborn woman. You're going to take this man upon yourself to cure. You are not God Almighty, in fact if you really want my opinion, he should be in a hospital."

"A hospital?" her strong voice came out incredulously shouting back at him. "No, never! Over my dead body, he'll never go to any of those monkey farms. If you aren't sick when you go in, all those people in white will make sure you die."

Abruptly showing him to the door, she opened it just short of saying come back someday when your medical science works! Complimenting herself on her self-control, she turned around and felt relieved that the likes of him was out of the house. Maybe she should open a window and air the place out. But she murmured instead.

"That's that, we tried bringing in medical science, now we'll begin the tried and true method."

She whisked her long black skirt around with one stroke and headed resolutely down the long hall toward the kitchen, bumping into Johnny on the way, causing him to turn.

"Where are you going in such a hurry, Ma? How is Dad doing?"

He stood looking after her. But he knew that determined look on his mother's face. Lips tightened, brown eyes straight ahead, she had a mission. And after seeing Dr. Stein drive away in a huff, he was perceptive enough, to realize what might have taken place.

Lizzie carefully unloaded all of her herbal remedies out of the cupboard and on to the sideboard. First, the large blue glass jar which held the precious tincture she had mixed at the end of summer, glad now they had taken the long ride into the country to see the Patterson's new house. Jim Patterson had stayed at the hotel five years ago, shortly after he married and moved to his new house in Monroeville. His wife Abigail, had a little garden plot set aside to grow herbs and had dried quite a few of them. She had also written down some remedial recipes which Lizzie had made at the end of August, using dried echinacea and goldenseal root, and myrrh powder with some cayenne, together with apple cider vinegar. This mixture had been stored on a dark shelf in the back of the pantry, allowing it to steep for the last couple of months. She hoped she'd remembered to shake the jar once in a while so that the herbs suspended in the alcohol as Abby had said. Now she carefully strained the mixture through a fine mesh cheesecloth, discarded the herbs and rebottled the tincture. She would spoon out some of this into Zach's tea a few times a day. Then she crushed fresh cloves of garlic with a mortar and pestle to mix with butter into thick spreadable paste, which released a flow of pungent fragrances all over the hotel.

"Is Lizzie making sausages today?" one hotel patron asked, breathing deeply.

"Nah," Phil retorted. "Ma's busy in her lab back dare, she's gonna knock da sox offa medical science taday."

Most of the men sitting around the bar laughed, but most knew her to be a woman of determination, especially when one of her own kind was down and out.

"Boy, the bar sure looks strange without Zach behind it. How's he doin' anyway? Even ole Phil's workin' for a change." One Westinghouse worker inquired. "Looks like he's goin' down with the country. Hey, whatdaya think of this new guy Roosevelt? I wonder if he can put some bandages on the country's problems."

Johnny, overhearing them while polishing some glasses from behind the bar said, "Well, I think he's a good man. He just got reelected governor unanimously in New York State and you know he helped the farmers out with tax relief. The only thing that bothers me is he's supporting Al Smith. The country isn't ready to elect a Catholic."

Most of the customers nodded their heads in agreement, not surprised that Johnny would bring up the religion issue.

"Da Mickeys in dis country are gonna have dere day yet," Phil growled. "What da hell does everyone have against 'em, burnin' da crosses, da damn klu kluckers out dere in 'ere nighties."

"Yeah, and the day we see ye in the Lord's house, Phil me boy, Jesus will be a'comin' down from the cross," Jerry O'Flaherty's Irish brogue broke in. Laughter erupted among the patrons, leaving Phil with a red face, knowing he rarely attended church.

Now what the hell were they bringin' him? He lucidated, in his weakened state, spying the door opening slowly. In what seemed like weeks, he'd been mustard-plastered, goose-greased and wrapped in flannel, sponged off with cool water during his delirium and fed liquids, from an awful tasting tea to chicken soup by the gallon. Scratching his sharp whiskers, he ran his fingers through them, mentally measuring how many days growth would have to be clean-shaved. Dell crept slowly around the front of the bed with a tray, viewing him hesitantly, as though he would rise from the dead at any time.

"What do you think Dell, should they ship me to the Carnegie Museum, maybe put me in a glass case on display or something?"

Her laughter made him feel good. Maybe things had been going better between her and Lizzie during the sick limbo he'd been in. Dell put his tray down, grabbing his pillows from behind him.

"Here, let's prop you up for your breakfast." She smelled of lavender, as her arm brushed against his face.

"Listen kid, could you get me a mirror first, I have to see what damage has been done to my mussey."

"Johnny is starting work as a Security Guard next week," she announced excitedly.

"And we're going to have another baby, maybe it'll be a girl this time. We figure we can finally move into a home at the end of the year."

"Good for you, Dell." When he held out his hand to commend her, she noticed how soft and thin it felt, almost like a fragile woman's hand. But his strong warmth poured through to her and she was glad he was back with them. Thank God their prayers had been answered. He lay back against the crisp fresh pillow Dell had placed behind him with her loving gentle hands, and closed his tired eyes, remembering a current poem, he'd liked enough to memorize.

Again the woods smell sweet.
The soaring larks lift up with them
the sky, which to our shoulders was so heavy;
true, through the boughs one still saw the day, how

empty it was,
but after long, rain-filled afternoons
come the golden sun-drenched newer hours,
before which, on distant housefronts,
all the wounded windows flee fearfully with beating wings.
Then it grows still. Even the rain runs more softly
over the stone's quietly darkening gleam.
All noises slip entirely away
into the brushwood's glimmering buds.

It was springtime and he and Lizzie were strolling hand in hand over the soft earth through Fairmount Park beside the Schuylkill. The penetrating flavors of spring filled their noses and lungs with stimulating sensations on the threshold of fresh growth. Lizzie was talking ambitiously about her plans to open a hotel. Zach loved discovering the new pink and white buds of dogwood and evergreens on the hillside planted the year before, pondering the miracle of their survival over the harsh winter. As they reached a thicket, he stepped off the path to rescue a wild rose vine that had wrapped itself around a young willow tree. Setting it free, he changed the course of the vine.

"Life is difficult for the new ones," he said. If we don't help them they'll get choked out by nature."

"Aw, but in some gardens they both grow happily and lovingly together," Lizzie replied smiling."

BIBLIOGRAPHY

This Fabulous Century, 1920, Volume III 1930 by the Editors of Time-Life Books, 1969

Maxwell Motor Company, Inc., Detroit, Michigan

Culture as History, The Transformation of American Society in the Twentieth Century, by Warren I. Susman, Pantheon Books, NY

Those Wonderful Old Automobiles, by Floyd Clymer, Bonanza Books, New York Division of Crown Publishers, Inc. with McGraw-Hill Book Co.

Great Times, An Informal Social History of the United States, 1914-1929, by J.C. Furnas, G.P Putnam's Sons

Czechoslovakia—A Country Study, Copyright 1989, US Government as represented by Secretary of the Army Louis R. Mortimer, Acting Chief Federal Research Division

The Priest, by Don Gold, published by Holt, Reinhart and Winston

The Day America Crashed, by Tom Shachtman, Putnam, NY

The Day the Bubble Burst, by Gordon Thomas and Max Morgan-Witts, A social history of the Wall Street Crash of 1929, Doubleday & Co., Inc., Garden City, NY

Modern Bride, The Complete Wedding Planner for Today's Bride, by Cele Goldsmith Lalli and Stephanie H. Dahl, John Wiley & Sons, Inc.

ABOUT THE AUTHOR

Elizabeth Lydia Bodner was born and raised in Pennsylvania. Upon graduating from California University of Pennsylvania, she moved to New England, where she met her husband Jim Cumiskey.

She and her husband relocated with his business several times. During these years away, she tenaciously wrote a composite of stories related by her parents regarding the early life and times of her grandmother's hotel.